Liz Isaacson

ISBN-13: 978-1542797078

ISBN-10: 1542797071

"Offer the sacrifices of righteousness, and put your trust in the Lord."

~Psalms 4:5

Chapter One

The possibilities had never been so wide open for Heidi Duffin. Though she needed a job—and quickly—she had four applications out, only one year remaining until she earned her Bachelor's degree in Baking and Pastry Arts, and a whole summer to enjoy herself.

"Why are we driving out here again?" Heidi peered into the nothingness surrounding her as her younger sister aimed their truck east down the middle of the two-lane highway.

"It's the first dance of summer in Three Rivers," Maggie said. "And Chase will be there."

Heidi frowned, her mind whirring to try to remember who Chase was. She couldn't. "And he's…?"

"He's the boy I met a couple of weeks ago in Daddy's store." Maggie glanced at Heidi, her fingers flexing on the steering wheel. "The cowboy?"

Realization lit up Heidi's mind at the same time her frown deepened. "Oh, yes. The cowboy."

"You don't have to say it like that." Maggie made her chuckle sound light, but Heidi knew annoyance sat just below the surface. "We aren't all big city girls." Maggie lifted her chin and pressed a bit harder on the accelerator. "I like cowboys."

"And apparently driving an hour for a dance." Heidi brushed something invisible from her skirt. "He must be something special."

Maggie giggled, and Heidi was reminded of the three-year difference in their ages. "He is. You meet anyone in San Francisco?"

Heidi had been grilled by her mother, and her grandmother, and then each of her mother's three sisters. As if she needed to find a handsome chef before she finished her own journey through culinary school. As if that was the only way to have value as a woman, even though it was nineteen-eighty-six and lots of women were joining the workforce these days.

And there had been Westin….

She shook her head, dislodging the dark eyes that always seemed so angry, and said, "No, I'm too busy baking to be dating."

"Oh, come on, Heidi. Surely you don't bake all day and all night."

She sighed. "No, but some days it feels like it." And she wouldn't have it any other way, despite the aching back and sore feet. Heidi was destined to have her own bakery someday, and she would. She absolutely would. She'd thought of little else for the past two years as she went to school in San Francisco, little else for the four years it had taken her to work and save for culinary school, little else since she was thirteen years old.

"So tell me about Chase," she said to get the questions away from her.

"He's a wrangler at the Three Rivers Ranch, and he is *soo* cute," Maggie singsonged. Heidi smiled at the exuberance of her sister. Of the three she had, Maggie was Heidi's favorite. The next youngest, Bridgette, had just graduated from high school and had started cosmetology school a week ago.

The baby of the family, Kayla, still had a couple years of high school left. Heidi loved all her sisters, but she and Maggie had been through the most together, caused the most trouble, and though they were practically opposites, Heidi got along great with her. Plus, Maggie had always helped out the most when their mom had to teach piano lessons late.

The two girls had put dinner on the table every Monday, Tuesday, and Wednesday night, and sometimes more if Momma went to help Daddy at the store. He owned and operated a farming supply store, which made it possible for Maggie to meet boys like Chase.

If their daddy knew that, though…he might close his doors. Heidi let the smile she felt show on her face. She loved her parents, and they'd worked hard to provide a good life for her and her sisters. Though she'd saved and scrimped, her parents had helped pay for pastry school. And heaven knew that wasn't cheap.

Thank you, she sent heavenward, the way she had everyday for the past two years. Gratitude filled her as signs of a town finally came into view.

"Oh, thank goodness," she said, picking at her pink mini-skirt again. "I thought we'd never get here."

"It's not that far," Maggie said as she slowed and entered the town of Three Rivers. "The dance is in the park." She leaned forward as if the giant windshield didn't provide an adequate view of her destination.

She turned here and there, and the streets became choked with cars and trucks. "Is the whole town coming to this dance?" Heidi peered out her window.

"Probably," Maggie said. "Chase said it was a big deal—the first dance of the summer, Heidi!"

"Yeah, first dance."

"Chase said the only event that's bigger is the Fourth of July celebration. Rodeos, picnics, parades. He says he's gonna come pick me up for that."

"Great," Heidi deadpanned. "You already got the weekend off?"

"No," Maggie said airily. "But Bridgette will cover for me if I need her to."

"Bridgette just started school," Heidi reminded her. "She hasn't been home before ten o'clock in the past week."

Something akin to panic raced across Maggie's face. "Kayla, then."

"You haven't told Daddy about Chase, have you?"

Maggie pulled behind another truck, the park nowhere in sight. "We'll have to walk."

"Maggie," Heidi warned.

"No," she said. "Okay? No, I haven't told Momma or Daddy about Chase."

"Where do they think we are?"

"Oh, I told them we were coming out to the dance here in Three

Rivers." She slid Heidi a mischievous grin that usually led to them being up a creek without a paddle. Literally, that had happened once after a cocked eyebrow like the one Maggie wore now. "I just didn't say why."

Heidi didn't want to grin at her sister, but she did, feeling younger than she had in a long time. "Okay, well, I can't wait to meet Chase."

Terror tamped out the excitement in Maggie's face. "Surely you'll find someone to dance with."

Heidi stared at her sister. "What do you mean? I came with you."

"I don't want you to meet Chase," Maggie blurted. "He'll like you more than me."

Heidi blinked, blinked. "What?"

Maggie's eyes rounded and she fiddled her fingers around each other. "You're prettier than me. And the boys always like you more."

Heidi burst into laughter, her sister's worry ridiculous. "That only happened once, and only because Elliot was a senior and was embarrassed to admit he liked a freshman."

It was Maggie's turn to blink and say, "What?"

"Yeah, that's what he told me at prom. That he really wanted to ask you, but you were too young." Heidi tossed a dry look to Maggie. "It wasn't my best date." She climbed out of the truck and took a deep breath of the fresh air. She'd give Three Rivers a nod for that. "So don't worry, Mags. I won't steal Chase from you."

They walked the two blocks to the park, where the country

music could be heard after the first block. Maggie swept the crowd, looking for the one face she knew, while Heidi hung behind her. She didn't know anyone here, and she didn't really care to.

"Maggie!" a man called, and both Heidi and Maggie swung in the direction it came from. A blond cowboy pushed through the crowd and swept a giggling Maggie off her feet. His blue eyes sparkled with laughter and he slung his arm around her shoulders as they faced Heidi.

"Chase, this is my sister," Maggie said, an edge of anxiety riding in her eyes. "Heidi."

"Nice to meet you, Miss Heidi." Chase grinned and extended his hand toward Heidi. She shook it, and shuffled her feet as he turned back to Maggie and started talking.

"I'll see you later, okay?"

Heidi yanked her gaze back to Maggie. "Later?"

"Yeah, I'm gonna go dance with Chase." She squealed and spun, leaving Heidi alone in this completely foreign place. Though, for a small town, this dance was impressive. She wandered along the edges of the dance floor until she ran into the refreshment table.

"Love your skirt," a girl said, a genuine smile on her face.

"Thanks," Heidi said as she plucked a cup of red punch off the table.

"Where'd you get it?"

"San Francisco." Heidi took a sip of punch, wishing her voice didn't carry a note of pride. She wasn't better than this girl, despite her fashionable mini-skirt and oversized top with a teal stripe along the neckline.

"Do you live there?" the girl asked. "Oh, I'm Farrah."

"Nice to meet you." Heidi smiled at her. "No, I don't live there. I'm going to school there."

Farrah got a faraway look on her face. "I wish I could go to school."

A pang of sadness hit Heidi, along with a wave of gratitude and the memories of her own longing to attend school. She'd worked for her father for four long years, living at home and spending nothing, until she could pay for the first year of culinary school.

"I'm sorry," she murmured, wanting to escape from this conversation. Though the sun had started to set, it suddenly felt too hot to Heidi. "Excuse me."

She turned, and everything seemed to happen in slow motion. Someone bumped her elbow—or maybe she bumped them. No matter what, her punch went flying, the red liquid practically leaping from the cup and flying through the air.

It hit the man who'd just stepped out of the crowd, and time rushed forward again. Heidi gasped at the same time the punch touched the man. He flinched like she'd physically touched him, and glanced down at his now-stained shirt.

His now-stained *white* shirt.

Heidi brought both hands to cover her mouth, absolutely horrified. "I'm so sorry," she said through her fingers. "I got hit, and—"

"It's okay," he said, his voice low and deep and wonderful and flowing like honey over Heidi's frayed nerves. The music faded into silence; the world narrowed to just the two of them.

She slid her eyes from his shirt and up his thick chest, taking in muscular arms under his short sleeves, and over the most handsome face she'd ever seen. He had a shock of dark hair poking out from beneath a black cowboy hat, and bright, electric blue eyes that drew her in like a magnet. He looked like he hadn't shaved in a couple of days, and the facial hair added to his allure.

His belt buckle could've served as a dinner plate, and at the bottom of his long, jean-clad legs, he wore a weathered pair of cowboy boots.

Heidi forgot her own name. She swallowed and dropped her hands back to her sides. All her mind could conjure was, *Maybe cowboys aren't so bad.*

"I don't think we've met." The man moved forward a step and reached for her. No, past her, to the refreshment table, where he collected a napkin and starting dabbing at his ruined shirt. "I'm Frank Ackerman."

Heidi startled and cleared her throat. "Heidi Duffin."

"You new in town, Heidi?" He settled his weight away from her, but his near proximity rendered her weak. He smelled like leather and pine and wood and everything manly and nice.

She took a deep breath of him, wanting to bake him into a pie so the aroma would infect the air for a long time. "Yes. I mean, no." She took a step back to give herself some air. "No, I don't live here. I'm just here with my sister." She scanned the crowd, half-hoping Maggie would appear to corroborate her story. "I guess she's dating some guy from some ranch—"

"Three Rivers Ranch?"

"Yeah, that's it." Heidi found his face again and smiled at him. When he returned the gesture, she thought sure she'd faint. She wondered if he knew how handsome he was, how fast her heart was racing, how he affected girls. "Anyway, I'm from Amarillo," she finished.

"You wanna dance?" He nodded his hat toward the dance floor.

Heidi hadn't intended to dance with anyone. Her brain screamed at her to say no. Her heart reminded her how she felt about cowboys, about living so far from civilization, about belt buckles the size of hubcaps.

But her voice said, "Sure," and a thrill of excitement tripped down her spine when Frank put his warm hand on the small of her back and guided her through the crowd.

Frank didn't know the pretty little woman who'd splashed punch down his chest, but he wanted to. Heidi had a calming voice, and though his shirt was starting to stick to his skin, he couldn't risk leaving her to clean up before he had a chance to dance with her. Someone else would pounce on a pretty woman like her.

She sported light brown hair the color of the river rocks out at Frank's ranch. Well, not really *his* ranch. At least not yet. As the eldest of three brothers, the ranch was being passed to him at the end of the year. He'd been knee-deep in figuring out how to run a twenty thousand acre cattle ranch without the help of his father.

Frank wanted the ranch, always had. That wasn't the problem. But he also wanted someone to run it with, and therein sat the biggest problem of Frank's life. His mother had died a decade ago, and Frank had seen how a ranch as vast and busy as Three Rivers could swallow a man. He'd watched his father disappear behind the desk, vanish out on the range, become a ghost in his own house.

Frank didn't want to be like his father. He wanted his life to be as vibrant as the ranch itself, full of laughter and family and food. And to do that, he needed a good woman who could introduce that spirit the way his mom had.

He'd been trying to find her for the past six months. Of course, he hadn't told any of the women he'd dated that, but he'd never made it that far in his relationships. He kept that desire close to the vest, worried it might scare a woman away.

As Heidi turned and slipped herself easily into his arms, he couldn't help picturing her out at Three Rivers. The thought brought a smile to his lips, and he gazed down into her more-brown-than-hazel eyes and found strength there.

"So what do you do in Amarillo?" he asked as the band started a mid-tempo tune he could twirl and hold Heidi to.

"Oh, I don't really live in Amarillo."

"No?"

"Well, I do, but I don't." She giggled, but quickly smothered it.

"Well, that makes all kinds of sense," he teased.

"My family lives there. I'm just home for the summer. I'm going to school in San Francisco."

Frank's heart dipped down to his boots, where it stayed for a few beats before rebounding to his chest. "What're you studying?"

"Baking and pastry arts." She practically glowed, and Frank

itched to run his fingers down the side of her face. "I'm going to open a bakery after I graduate."

So she could cook. Frank liked a woman who knew her way around a kitchen. "That's great," he said, genuine about her baking, but not liking that she wouldn't be around very long. "What are you doin' this summer?"

"Trying to find a job." She possessed a quiet power, which called to Frank's soul.

"I can help with that," he said.

"Oh?" She gazed up at him with an open expression, her petite hand pressing into his shoulder warm and welcome.

"Sure," he said. "I heard Three Rivers Ranch needs someone to clean their cowboy cabins this summer."

She blinked, distracting him with her long lashes. "I'm sure that won't work."

"Why not?" Frank pulled his gaze from her and looked around as if he didn't mind if she turned him down. But he did. He wanted to see her everyday, get to know her better, and he couldn't drive to Amarillo at the drop of a hat. Or even once a week.

"Because I live in Amarillo." Her fingers inched down his arm, and Frank's stomach flipped.

"You could live on the ranch." What was he saying? He felt as if he was grasping for straws.

A beautiful blush stained her cheeks. "Do you live on the ranch, Mister Ackerman?"

He met her eye again, pleased by the ring of desire he saw there. "Well…." He didn't want to tell her he actually owned the ranch.

Or that he would in six months when his father signed everything over to him and made it official. He'd kept that information private for as long as possible too. Seemed once women discovered that he was about to become the owner of the ranch, they were doubly interested.

Sure, the ranch was profitable. Some would say he was rich. But he didn't want the ranch to be the reason someone liked him, and that had been happening more and more lately.

"Well, what?" Heidi pressed.

"Yeah, I live on the ranch."

"And you just happen to know that I could live out there and clean cabins?"

"Yes."

She cocked her head to the side, a cute gesture that only made Frank more interested in Heidi Duffin. "I'll think about it."

Which meant no. The song neared its end, and Frank felt frantic. She'd step away, melt into the crowd, and he'd never see her again. He wasn't sure what to do, and he offered a desperate prayer for help.

What do I say?

Nothing came to mind. The song ended, and sure enough, Heidi fell back. "Thank you for the dance, Mister Ackerman."

"Wait," he blurted as she started to turn. His eyes slid down her clothes, landing on her black sandals before bouncing back to her face. He couldn't just let her walk out of his life. "I need to get your phone number."

Her eyebrows shot toward her hairline. "You do?"

Thinking fast, he gestured to his ruined shirt. "Yeah. I'll need to send you a cleaning bill."

Horror washed over her face, and Frank immediately regretted his tactic to get her phone number. He just knew he couldn't let her walk away. He moved closer as another song started up, this one much louder and faster than the previous tune.

"Of course, if you let me take you down the street to the ice cream parlor, I could forget about the ruined shirt." He grinned at her, well aware of the power of his straight, white teeth and flirtatious tone.

She seemed as susceptible to his smile as most other women, a curve playing with her pink lips. Frank cleared his throat, aware he'd leaned closer and closer to her. Heidi looped her arm through his. "I love mint chocolate chip. Do they have that?"

He'd personally make her some if they didn't. "I'm sure they do." He led her off the dance floor, relief rushing through him with the force of river rapids. "I'm more of a praline and caramel kind of man myself."

"That's my daddy's favorite flavor," she said.

"He must be an amazing man, then."

Heidi practically wilted beside him, and Frank wondered if he'd struck gold by going to the dance tonight. He hadn't planned on coming. Didn't even want to. His cowhands would attend all summer long, but as the boss, Frank rarely went with them. Plus, his age set him apart from the crowd. And his status, his last attempt at a girlfriend had told him.

After Whitney had said every girl watched him wherever he

went, he'd stayed out at Three Rivers, only coming to town for church. He'd even been sending a cowhand—and paying him—to do his grocery shopping. Lots of women at the grocery store, and Frank didn't need them ogling him while he was trying to select the right variety of apple. Or hitting on him while he put milk in his cart. Or gossiping about when the thirty-year-old bachelor would find a wife and take over the ranch.

"Frank?"

"Hmm?" He returned to the warm evening, the weight of Heidi's fingers on his arm.

"I asked what you do for a living."

"Oh, uh." Frank's feet dragged against the cement. He didn't want to lie, but he didn't want to tell her either. "I'm out at the ranch." Not really a fib, if God didn't count omission as a lie.

"Oh, that's right. You like it? The life of a wrangler?"

"Yeah, it's great." Frank reached for the door handle and pulled. The bell on the ice cream parlor's door jingled and a woman lifted her head.

"Hey, Frank," she said with an obvious note of suggestion in her voice. Frank cursed himself for coming in, for not remembering that Victoria worked at the shop. They'd gone out a few times, right at the beginning of Frank's dating spree, and while Vickie was easy on the eyes, that was where her beauty ended.

"Evenin', Vickie." Frank tightened his arm against his side, keeping Heidi right next to him.

"Here for the flavor of the month?" Vickie's appraising gaze slid over Heidi. "Oh, it looks like you already found one."

Heat flamed in Frank's face. He hadn't intentionally tried to speed through several women in Three Rivers, but unfortunately he didn't need very many dates to decide if he liked someone or not.

Heidi's hand slipped out of his arm, and she put several steps between them as she moved up to the counter. "Do you have mint chocolate chip?" Her voice sounded on the upper range of her octave, though Frank had just met her and didn't know for certain.

"Yes." Vickie scooped with extra vigor while Frank glared, hoping she could feel the weight and displeasure in his gaze.

The next morning, Frank strode from the homestead through the yard to the cowboy cabins. He counted down six to Chase's, climbed the steps, and knocked on the door. Several seconds passed before the blond cowboy opened the door.

"Boss," he said, falling back a step in obvious surprise. "Come in." He swiped a cowboy hat from a hook on the wall and smashed it on his bedhead. "What brings you here this mornin'?" Chase yawned as he backed into the kitchen. "Coffee?"

Frank waved him away. "No, I'm fine, Chase." He glanced around the cabin, the questions he had obvious and embarrassing.

Chase busied himself making coffee anyway, and Frank realized he'd woken the cowboy on his only morning off this week. "Chase," he said. "I'm sorry. I just realized I woke you."

"It's fine." Chase tossed a smile over his shoulder. "I'm up now."

"I'll give you Monday morning off too."

Chase's grin widened. "Really?"

"Really."

"Great." He finished with the coffee and faced Frank. "So, what can I do for you?"

Frank cleared his throat. He'd always been able to just say what needed to be said. It was one of his greatest strengths. "The girl you met at the dance last night, what was her name?"

Chase's eyes narrowed. "Maggie."

"Maggie, right." Frank remembered that Heidi had said she had three sisters. "And she has sisters?"

"Yeah." Chase drew the word out, waiting, extreme curiosity burning through his eyes.

Frank dropped his gaze to his cowboy boots. "You have her phone number?" He'd left Heidi on the outskirts of the dance after they'd licked their cones gone and walked the perimeter of the park twice. He'd wanted to hold her hand while they walked, hug her good-bye, ask for her phone number himself, but Vickie's poisoned words had caused Heidi to put distance between them. She hadn't touched him again, a fact every cell in Frank's body had been mourning for the past ten hours.

"You want to call my girl?" The incredulity in Chase's voice hit Frank like a punch.

"No," he said quickly, lifting his eyes to his cowhand's. "No, of course not. Her sister. Maggie came to the dance last night with her sister, Heidi. I want to call her, but I wasn't able to get her number before they left."

Realization and relief sagged Chase's bunched shoulders. A knowing smile followed. "I saw you two dancing. She's pretty."

Frank wasn't interested in gossiping about Heidi's beauty. "So can I have the number?"

Chase got up and retrieved a slip of paper from his messy kitchen counter. "What are you gonna do? Just call her and...then what? What will you tell her about how you got her number?"

Frank didn't know, and he admitted as much to Chase. "Any ideas?" he asked.

"Maybe she won't ask," Chase said.

Frank knew she would. He didn't know everything about Heidi Duffin, but he'd seen the sharpness in her eyes, enjoyed the wit in their conversation, and he knew she was smart. "She'll ask," he said, his heart plummeting though Chase handed him the paper with the number written on it. "Maybe I'll just see if she applies for the housekeeping job."

But he knew she wouldn't. She'd made her position clear about living out at the ranch, calling Three Rivers "the middle of nowhere," and asking him if he liked living so far from the city.

She seemed his opposite in every way, and yet he'd barely been able to sleep for want of seeing her again, hearing her voice, answering her questions, learning all he could about her. He mashed the paper in his fist and stuffed it in his pocket. "Thanks, Chase."

"You'll think of something," Chase called as Frank opened the door and left the cabin. "Let me know how it goes!"

But Frank wouldn't. Because he wasn't going to call Heidi

Duffin and tell her he'd gone crawling to her sister's boyfriend to get her phone number. A phone number she hadn't chosen to give him.

Chapter Two

By the following Friday, when Maggie asked Heidi to drive to Three Rivers for another dance, Heidi's shoulders felt weighed down by stress. She still hadn't found a job, so she'd been helping at the store by sweeping and cleaning out the storage room.

But she wasn't getting paid, and she needed something that could put dollars in her bank account. She didn't work while in school, and she had expenses on top of tuition to pay for.

Frank's offer to work out at Three Rivers Ranch had crossed her mind at least once a day for the past week, and in the past few days, that frequency had increased to once an hour. Maggie had Chase's phone number, and it would be easy enough to get in touch with Frank if Heidi really wanted to.

And she did. But the implication from Vickie at the ice cream shop had left a bad taste in Heidi's mouth. She wasn't interested in being someone's flavor of the month. Before she'd met Frank, she hadn't been that interested in dating at all.

Now, he dominated her thoughts, his handsome face and easy laugh sneaking into her mind while she swept and organized and worried.

"So do you want to go?" Maggie pressed. "I saw you dance with that cowboy, and then you disappeared." She waggled her eyebrows at Heidi and then returned to applying her mascara. "You never told me where you went."

Heidi hadn't. Not only did she want to avoid her sister's teasing, she wasn't sure how she felt about Frank. She wanted to see him again, but not if he was seeing someone else every other week. Her chest pinched tight, tighter, and she released a breath.

"Yes, I'll come with you."

Maggie squealed and scanned Heidi's clothes. "You better change. Your handsome cowboy won't want to smell you wearing that."

Heidi glanced down at her overall shorts, dusty and dirty from the back corner of the supply closet she'd cleaned out that morning. "What should I wear?"

"Something cute, like last week. Oh, I know!" She leapt up from her vanity and reached for something in her closet. "You have those adorable black-and-white leggings. This will be killer with those." She held out a soft pink oversized sweatshirt, which Heidi eyed with doubt.

"That'll fall off my shoulder."

"It's supposed to do that." Maggie shook the hanger and Heidi took the garment. "And you can borrow my black heels. That'll get you closer to Frank's height."

Heidi's breath left her body, and she gasped for air. "How did you know his name?"

Maggie startled, and a blush crawled up her neck. "Um, well,

Chase told me that he came to get our number. Wondered if he'd called you." She finished with the powder and turned. "He hasn't called you, has he?"

Heidi shook her head, slow warmth spreading through her body. No, Frank hadn't called. But he'd wanted to. He'd gone to Maggie's boyfriend to get the phone number Heidi had been wishing for seven straight days she'd given him.

She shimmied into her leggings and spritzed perfume on her shoulders. "Did Chase say if Frank would be at the dance tonight?"

"He didn't. He told me on Sunday that he was surprised he was there last week."

"Why's that?" Heidi held out Maggie's sweatshirt and ducked her head into it.

Maggie shrugged. "I guess he never goes."

Heidi paused in her preparations. "Well, maybe he won't be there tonight, then." She really didn't want to hover near the punch table like she had last week unless the possibility of disappearing with Frank was high.

You don't want to disappear with him, *she scolded herself.* You just want to ask him about the job.

But if that were true, Heidi could've done it without driving the hour to Three Rivers. She could get Chase's number right now, call him, and ask how to get in touch with Frank. She didn't have to wear heels that pinched her pinky toes, or lipstick, or the insane hope that she'd see him again.

"You want me to call Chase?" Maggie offered. "Maybe he can let us know if Frank will be there or not. Get him to go or something."

Heidi seized onto the idea, because it was the best one they had. "Yes, call Chase."

Maggie bounced out of the room to the phone in the hall. She stretched the cord as far as it would go, which was just inside their bedroom door if she pulled really hard with one hand and kept the cord connected to the phone with the other.

Unease ran through Heidi's blood as her sister giggled and flirted with Chase after he picked up. When she finally said, "So, Chase, my sister is wondering if Frank will be at the dance tonight."

The pause stretched for far too long. Heidi slicked on a layer of dark red lipstick like she wasn't hanging on Maggie's every breath.

"She really wants to see him," Maggie finally said. "Maybe you could convince him to come with you." She grinned at Heidi. "Okay, see you soon." She returned the phone to its cradle and returned to the bedroom to flop on the bed. "He said he'd try to get Frank to go. I guess he'd already asked him, and Frank had said no, he wouldn't be going."

Panic raced through Heidi, though she had no idea why. She'd spent a few hours with the man. Sure, she'd felt comfortable in his presence, had enjoyed his laugh and his stories about his brothers. So he was handsome and kind and tall. He was also a cowboy, and that alone put a big black mark on him.

Or did it?

Heidi shivered at the thought of his large, capable hands holding hers, cupping her face before he kissed her. She blinked and hurried to shove her feet into Maggie's heels. She wasn't a schoolgirl, and she couldn't entertain such fantasies.

Still, Frank starred in her mind for the entire drive to Three Rivers.

Frank hadn't come to the dance. With every passing moment, Heidi's anxiety grew at the same time her hopes fell. Chase had grabbed Maggie almost from the moment they'd entered the park. She'd come running back to say he didn't know about Frank and hadn't been able to talk to him in person before leaving.

So Heidi had gotten her punch—and kept it in the cup this time—and found a spot on the fringes and hoped Frank had gotten the note Chase had left for him. She caught several men looking her way, but none of them interested her. Though they wore jeans like Frank, and belt buckles like Frank, and cowboy hats like Frank, they didn't hold a candle to Frank's charisma and personality.

She toyed with the idea of asking Chase for Frank's phone number and then somehow finding someplace to call him. But she told herself such thoughts bordered on desperate, and if there was one thing Heidi Duffin didn't want to be, it was desperate.

The shoes pinched, and she bent to take them off. She hooked her fingers through the straps and left the dance behind. The grass felt cool against her bare feet and as the bulk of the noise fell off, she took a deep, deep breath of the fresh country air.

With the sun down, the summer night air brushed coolly against her skin, and she tipped her chin to the rising moon. Peace descended on her, and Heidi felt more at home here, in this tiny town she'd visited twice, than she had in Amarillo. Even more than she had in San Francisco. The idea unsettled her so much that she found an empty bench as far from the dance as possible and sat down.

"I want to go home," she whispered, though the night was young and Maggie wouldn't be ready to go for hours yet. And Heidi didn't exactly know where home was. *That's all*, she thought as she realized why she felt so peaceful here in Three Rivers. She was just in transition right now and didn't feel settled anywhere.

"This seat taken?"

Heidi startled at the deep voice, recognizing it a moment later. "Frank," she breathed as her eyes found his through the dim light.

She started to stand at the same time he sat. She re-settled next to him, folding her hands into her lap, not quite sure what to say.

"I had to work late," he said as if she'd asked him where he'd been.

She'd been dying to talk to him all week, and now here he sat and she had nothing to say. Her fingers itched to touch his; she longed to take a deep breath of his cologne—or his aftershave, as his face was clean-shaven tonight.

"Your feet hurt?"

She glanced at him, nearly blinded by his handsomeness. "Hmm?"

He nodded to the shoes, and she jerked them up. "Oh, these. They're my sister's, and they—well, I'm not used to wearing heels." She tried for a carefree laugh and mostly managed it. "In the kitchen, I'm on my feet all day, so...." She flipped the shoes again. "They're cute, though."

He chuckled, the sound sending vibrations through the air, through Heidi's soul. She smiled as she felt the happiness in him. The sound tapered into silence, and she heard the melancholy notes in the absence too.

"So I guess dancin' is out for tonight," he said.

"I liked walking with you better."

"I don't know if that's a compliment or not."

She realized how her words sounded, and horror shot through her. "It's just that, you know, the music is so loud, I can barely hear myself think let alone hear you talking to me."

He tapped his booted toe to the music blaring from across the park. "Not much for loud music myself."

"Yeah, Chase said you weren't planning to come tonight."

"I wasn't."

"What changed your mind?"

He shrugged, his toe going still as he stared into the distance. "I don't know."

Heidi heard the slightest twang of a lie, and she hoped he'd come because Chase had left a note for him saying she'd be there.

"Well, I'm glad you did." She flashed him a quick smile and plucked up her courage. "Frank, I was wondering about the job out at the ranch."

He whipped his gaze to hers. "The job?"

"You know, cleaning cabins? Do you happen to know if it's still available?"

"Yes." He swallowed. "It's still available." He peered at her as if trying to peel back the layers of her brain to find her true meaning underneath. "You can't drive all the way out there everyday from Amarillo."

"You said I could live on the ranch."

"I did say that."

"Is it true?"

"Sure is."

"How do I apply?"

"Don't need to. You can come on out on Monday and get started. I'll show you around and everything."

Heidi frowned. "I don't need to interview or fill anything out?"

He waved his hand like such things had gone out of style. "Nah, nothing like that. Bring your driver's license and someone will get the paperwork done."

Surprise shot through Heidi, but she didn't want to turn down a job, especially one she'd barely had to try to get. "How much does it pay?"

"Is five dollars an hour all right?"

She almost choked. "Yes, that's just fine." It was more than fine. And a dollar more than anything she'd applied for in Amarillo—and would've been happy to get. "I have to leave at the end of August," she said.

Something strange crossed his face. Something like determination or regret. Or both. "Okay," he said.

Her heart stuttered, suddenly doubting her decision to move out to Three Rivers Ranch to work for the summer, even if it meant she could be closer to Frank. If he really was "okay" with her leaving at the end of the summer, maybe he really did date a new woman every month. And she didn't want to be one of them, just another name in a long list of women Frank Ackerman had charmed.

Because the man was as charming as the day was long. Just sitting next to him had her nerves standing straight like soldiers. And yet, something about him put her at ease too.

"Tell me about pastry school," he said. "What kinds of things do you do there?"

She watched him for a sign of teasing, a bit of sarcasm, and found none. "Well, we learn how to bake. We take a lot of menu planning courses, and business classes, but mostly, we cook."

"Cook what?"

"Cakes and cookies. Crème anglaise. Puddings. Trifles. Anything and everything. We study cookbooks and memorize recipes." Her voice grew animated. Oh, how Heidi loved to be in the kitchen, a carton of eggs nearby and the steam rising from a double-boiler behind her.

They talked and talked, right there on the bench. Frank played the part of perfect gentleman, his laugher quick and his smiles sincere. His questions endless, and his voice the most soothing thing Heidi had heard in a long time.

Finally, a shadowy pair began to approach them. "That's my sister," Heidi said, getting to her feet. The night had grown the teensiest bit chilly, and she shivered as Frank stood too, positioning himself close enough to her that his body warmth touched her skin.

Feeling brave and bold, she stretched up and kissed his cheek. “I’m glad you came,” she whispered. Her sister drew closer and closer still. “And I hope you’ll use that phone number you got from Chase.”

She ducked away from him, intercepting Maggie before she got too close to Frank. She hooked her elbow through her sister’s and pulled her in the opposite direction. “Come on, let’s go.”

“Why?” Maggie glanced over her shoulder as she stumbled along beside Heidi. “He’s just standing there like a statue. What did you say to him?”

“Nothing,” Heidi mumbled though her chest felt like a swarm of birds had decided to hold a party inside.

“Let me say good-bye to Chase first.” Maggie unlinked their arms and threw herself into Chase’s arms. Heidi looked away as they kissed, her gaze landing on Frank. One hand touched his cheek where she’d kissed him.

When he saw her turned in his direction, he dropped his hand. She lifted hers in a wave good-bye, and he reciprocated. Maggie returned, and Heidi hurried away from Frank before he could hear her schoolgirl giggle.

“You’re gonna have to tell her who you are,” Frank told his reflection on Sunday morning before church. “When she gets here tomorrow, she’ll want to see the boss.” He jabbed one finger at the mirror. “And you’re the boss now.”

"Stop talkin' to yourself and get out of the bathroom," his brother, Ben, called from the other side of the door.

Frank turned away and yanked open the door. "I wasn't talkin' to myself."

"I heard you." Ben threw him a smirk as he entered the bathroom and gently pushed Frank into the hall. "Don't leave me this time. I'll be ready in fifteen minutes."

"I'm leavin' in twelve," Frank threatened as the door slammed closed. Ben was always running just a few minutes late, a pet peeve of Frank's. His father had taught him to be on time, that it showed respect to whoever might be waiting on him to arrive. He'd made it a habit to arrive fifteen minutes early for everything. That way, no one was ever waiting for him.

Well, Heidi was still waiting for that phone call. Frank had learned that Chase had told Maggie about Frank asking for Heidi's number. He felt thrown back to junior high, when he had to pass notes to find out if a girl liked him.

Being thirty, single, and about to inherit the biggest cattle ranch in the Texas Panhandle wasn't much easier, in Frank's honest opinion. And he didn't want Heidi to know about the last part.

"But you're gonna tell her this afternoon," he mumbled to himself as he went upstairs. "When you call her."

"Call who?" TJ asked.

"No one," Frank practically barked. He really needed to stop talking to himself. "You goin' to church like that?"

TJ glanced down at his pajamas—a pair of grungy sweat pants and a T-shirt with last week's dinner spilled on it. "Not goin' to church."

Frank watched his brother head downstairs, at a loss for what to do for TJ. He hadn't been to church in several months, though Frank asked him every week. TJ preferred sleeping in on Sundays, or lounging around with a bowl of popcorn and a stack of video cassettes, or disappearing out on the range with nothing but a horse, a bottle of water, and enough common sense not to get lost, though Frank was starting to doubt the last bit.

Sighing, he continued into the galley-style kitchen, where his father stirred oatmeal at the stove. Always oatmeal, every morning. Frank hated the stuff. But his mother had made oatmeal the day she died, and something about it calmed his dad, almost like he could still see her, be with her, when he made the meal she'd eaten last.

"Mornin', Dad." Frank pulled open the fridge and grabbed the near-empty juice pitcher. He retrieved a can from the freezer and proceeded to make more. "You want to ride to church with me and Ben?"

"Yeah, he wants to go to the picnic afterward." His dad glanced up from the pot. "Wants me to meet his Rebecca."

"Ah." Frank smiled. "You'll like her." He poured himself a tall glass of orange juice, about the best treat he could imagine, especially first thing in the morning.

"So he'll probably get married before you."

Frank nearly choked on his juice. "I guess so." He hadn't heard Ben talking marriage with Rebecca, but he knew they were serious—especially if Ben wanted Dad meet her. "Does it matter?"

"'Course not. Ranch is still yours."

"Ben doesn't want the ranch anyway."

"I know." He scooped oatmeal into a bowl. "He thinks he'll open a practice in Dallas after he finishes dental school."

"Probably wise." Frank had been telling Ben to do that for years. Something about Three Rivers called to Ben, but with a dentist already in town, it made it hard for him to stay. Frank had the ranch, and TJ had one year of college left before earning his environmental engineering degree. He and Ben would graduate at the same time, and then they'd both be gone.

Frank's youngest brother, Miles, lived and worked construction in Wyoming. Frank hadn't seen him in a year. Though he'd left on friendly terms, he wasn't interested in returning to the ranch.

Frank glanced around the run-down kitchen, his dreams for a bigger, newer homestead blooming in his mind. He'd been meaning to talk to his father about it for a while now. He took a deep breath to start, but Ben came bustling into the kitchen, whistling loudly. "See? Fifteen minutes."

"Time to go, then." Frank set his glass in the sink to wash later. "Ready, Dad?" The three of them barely fit in the tiny kitchen, and Frank stepped toward the front door while he waited for his dad to answer.

He swallowed one more bite of oatmeal. "Ready."

"You're coming to the picnic?" Ben asked. "You know we're going after church, right? Did you tell him, Dad?"

"I told 'im."

Frank grinned at Ben. "I'm fine to stay for the picnic."

Ben narrowed his eyes, searching for something Frank had hidden deep. "But you never stay for the picnic."

"Who says I'm stayin' today?" He moved into the living room and opened the front door.

"You did. Just now." Ben let Dad go by. "What's goin' on?"

"I said I'd stay. I didn't say I'd go." The very thought sent shivers—and not the good kind—down his spine. All those people. All those eyes. All those women.... No, Frank would not be attending the picnic. But he could make a phone call while Ben and his dad went. He'd just sneak back over to the church and use the line there. The pastor wouldn't mind, and Frank would have some privacy.

"It's a couple of hours." Ben looked out the open front door. "I could drive Dad in his truck."

"I'm good." Frank smiled at his brother in what he hoped was a reassuring gesture. The thought of coming back to the house alone didn't sit well, and neither did driving to town alone.

"Okay," Ben said. "But I don't want you flagging us down from the sidewalk too early."

"I won't." Frank gestured for Ben to exit. "I promise," he added when his brother wouldn't move. Ben finally stepped outside, and Frank followed, pulling the door closed behind him. He noticed the warped wood, the way the house needed to be repainted, the overgrown state of the yard. It all needed an overhaul, and though he didn't have time to dedicate to the homestead, he wanted to. How could he ever expect a woman to come live with him out here in such conditions?

She'd want an upgrade, to be sure. A dishwasher at the very least. Frank made a mental note to talk to his father that night. Not to let another day go by without at least asking if they had the money to make the house a home again.

The drive to town reminded Frank of how much he loved Texas, how settling the clear, blue sky could be, how far Heidi would have to drive to work.

He managed to put her from his mind long enough to listen to Pastor Allan's message about sacrifice. He spoke of Abraham and Isaac, a story that had always held a special place in Frank's heart. The sermon sank into his heart, and gratitude filled his whole soul.

Afterward, he whispered to Ben, "I'll meet you guys over at the park," and loitered in the chapel while it emptied. Finally, only he and Pastor Allan remained.

"How are you, Frank?"

"Doin' great."

"How are things at the ranch?" The man stood just about six feet tall, same as Frank, and exuded kindness. Frank had never had any problems feeling the sincerity in the pastor's questions. He'd never been afraid to talk about hard things, or something he struggled with. Some people were born to be certain things. Pastor Allan was one of them. Frank thought he was too—he'd only ever wanted to be a cowboy, a horseman, a rancher. It ran in his blood, the same way preaching ran in Pastor Allan's.

"Okay," Frank said. "I need to talk to my father about doing some upgrades on the homestead."

"Oh?" The pastor pointed over his shoulder. "You want to

come sit in my office while we talk?"

"Sure." Frank followed him through the lobby and down the hall to his office.

"What's wrong with the homestead?" The pastor settled behind his desk and pulled some paperwork toward him.

"Nothing's really *wrong* with it." Frank bumped up his hat and scrubbed the back of his head. "But it was my momma who really kept it up. Dad's…well, Dad's focused on getting the ranch ready to turn over to me, and he's never really paid much attention to the house."

"And you do?"

"I think my wife would." The words left Frank's mouth before he could think. His throat tightened, but Pastor Allan didn't seem to notice that he'd said anything peculiar.

"Are things getting serious with someone?" he asked.

"No," Frank said quickly. "And that leads me to why I stayed after." He chuckled, and it sounded nervous to his own ears. "There's a woman who lives in Amarillo I need to call." He dug her number out of his front pocket. The paper had been smashed and crinkled and smoothed a hundred times. "Can I use the phone here? My brother and dad are at the picnic, and well." Another chuckle. "That's not really my idea of a fun Sunday afternoon."

The pastor laughed. "I completely understand." He pushed the phone closer. "You talk as long as you want." He stood and stepped around the desk. "Unfortunately, my wife thinks the picnic is the best use of time for a Sunday afternoon. I'll see you next week, Frank." He stepped out of the office, closing the door behind him, and leaving Frank with no further impediments to calling Heidi.

Why then, was his stomach rioting against him? Why did his fingers tremble the slightest bit as he pressed the buttons to dial? Why couldn't he seem to inflate his lungs all the way?

"Hello?" a man answered, cementing this as the hardest phone call Frank had ever made.

"Yes, hello," he said, his own voice ringing in his head. "Is Heidi there? This is Frank Ackerman, and I need to give her some information about the job out at Three Rivers Ranch?"

He pressed his eyes closed as regret laced through him. He needed to give her information about the job? When she'd whispered that he use the number he'd gotten from Chase, Frank knew it wasn't to call and give her information about any job.

"Just a moment, please," her father said, and Frank exhaled.

With every passing moment, he felt sure he should hang up. But an iron will kept his grip on the receiver sure, and soon enough, Heidi said, "Frank?"

"Hey, Heidi," he breathed. "How are you? I didn't interrupt anything, did I?"

She giggled. "No, of course not."

The smile she wore in her voice caused his insides to warm, to turn to honey, golden and thick. "Unless you count Daddy starting to lecture Maggie about using so much gas."

"You still comin' out to the ranch tomorrow?"

Scuffling came through the line, and when she spoke again, her voice seemed thinner, higher, almost stretched across the distance between them. "Yes, and that's another thing you've interrupted."

A blip of anxiety bounced through him. "Oh?"

"My father owns the farming supply store here in Amarillo, right? Well, he said I can just work there. That I don't need to move out to Three Rivers to work."

All of Frank's hopes and dreams nosedived. "Oh."

"I told him I was going anyway."

Frank's eyebrows lifted. "Oh?"

"Is that all you can say?" She laughed again, and Frank thought the sound of her voice could paint beautiful pictures.

"No," he said. "I'm listening. So you're still coming out tomorrow?"

"Yes. Maggie is going to drive me and all my stuff. So I won't have a car out there. Is that a problem?"

"Not at all," Frank said. "We have lots of ranch vehicles."

"Ranch vehicles a woman can take into town to buy groceries?"

"Yeah, sure."

"And you're authorized to let me use one of these vehicles?" The interest in her voice didn't escape him, and the perfect opportunity to tell her about his role on the ranch had presented itself.

"Yes," he said slowly. "Heidi, there's something you should know. I *own* Three Rivers Ranch." He held his breath while he waited for her to respond.

"You—oh."

"Look who's saying it now." He chuckled, though he still didn't feel out of the woods. "I guess I should've told you, but well, I haven't been real lucky with women once they find out." And in Three Rivers, everyone already knew he'd eventually become the owner. They just didn't know when. The fact that he'd thought he could find someone to marry in town was laughable.

"Why's that?"

He decided to be honest, straightforward. It had never failed him. "They tend to like the idea of me more than me," he said. "You know, because of all the land and money and...whatever."

"You have a lot of land and money?"

"Yes, ma'am."

She laughed, and he imagined her with her head tipped back, that luxurious brown hair falling over her shoulders and down her back, the column of her neck exposed and begging to be kissed.

He cleared his throat as she said, "I'm hardly old enough to be called ma'am."

"That's another thing I need to come clean about," he said.

"Oh?" She made her voice deep like his as she copied him.

He smiled, happiness coursing through him in waves. "How old are you, Heidi?"

"Twenty-four."

"Okay, so I'm older than that."

"How much older than that?"

"Come Halloween, I'll be seven years older than that."

"Oh, well, that's...that's nothing. A single dog year."

"I own dogs too," he said. "Two of them."

"You've mentioned them before," she said, that smile still evident in her tone. "Duke and Daisy, if I remember right."

"You do." He took a deep breath. "So, you see, I'll be showing you around the ranch and signing your paychecks and everything, and I didn't want you to be blindsided by that when you come tomorrow."

"Thank you for telling me." After a pause, she added, "So you really did call about the job."

"No." He chuckled. "But what would you like me to tell your father next time I call?"

"There won't be a next time," she said.

"Oh, right. Because next time I want to talk to you, I can just stop by your house." The thought made his stomach dance with excitement.

"Right. Frank?"

"Yeah?"

"Is the cabin—I mean, I'm sure it's fine. But maybe you can tell me about it."

His temperature rose a couple of degrees. If he wanted to keep Heidi out at the ranch, he'd definitely need to invest in some upgrades. "The cabins aren't much," he confessed. "But they're not bad either. Yours has new appliances and fresh paint." He continued to tell her about the cabins, the ranch, the job, himself. A half hour later, she said her father was threatening to pull the cord from the wall if she didn't get off the phone, and they said their good-byes.

Frank replaced the receiver in the cradle and stared at it. He'd dated his fair share of women, and none of them—*none* of them—made his heart pound the way Heidi Duffin did. None of them interested him the way she did. None of them sang to his soul as strongly as she did.

And he didn't know what to do next. His other relationships he'd ended. But this one needed to continue, and that was all new territory for Frank.

He decided he'd do what Abraham had done. He'd pack up and climb the mountain, constantly praying for God to guide him, keep him, save him.

Chapter Three

"I can't believe *you're* going to live out here," Maggie said as she turned from paved road to dirt.

"You don't have to say it like that." Nerves had been rippling through Heidi since she woke that morning. Maybe even since the previous night.

"Like what?"

"Like I'm a city girl who hates the country."

"Heidi, you are a city girl who hates the country."

Heidi lifted her chin. "That's not true. I love this wide open sky. And the fields on the way out have been wonderful."

"Do they have phones out here?" Maggie peered through the windshield like they'd entered a foreign country. In many ways, Heidi felt like they had.

"Of course. Frank called me yesterday." But now she wondered. Did every cabin have a phone? Or would she have to call her family in public?

Not that she planned to call that much. She'd argued with her father for most of Saturday, finally clinching it with, "Daddy, I worked for you for a full week and you never once offered to pay me. He's paying me five dollars an hour."

"Five dollars?" her father had asked. And that had been the winning argument. That, and free housing. Her family was used to living without her. They wouldn't miss her. Well, maybe Maggie.

"I can't believe you're living out here," she said as she rounded a bend and the homestead and ranch buildings came into view. "I'm so jealous!"

"I won't steal Chase," she said for at least the twentieth time.

"I want phone calls as often as you can make them," she said as she parked in an open spot in front of a long, metal building that housed animals. Chickens and calves, by the looks of it.

"I want to know everything that happens with Frank Ackerman." Maggie giggled even though her eyes remained serious. They'd hashed through his conversation for an hour after Heidi had hung up, and she suspected she'd need her sister's help in navigating a relationship with him. After all, she'd never really been more than friends with a man.

And she definitely wanted to be more than friends with Frank.

Someone knocked on her window, and she jumped, her heart skyrocketing and her adrenaline spiking. She clutched both hands to her throat as she stared into Frank's vibrant blue eyes.

His laughter came through the glass, and she shoved the door open, which caused him to step back. "You devil." She swatted at his biceps. "You scared me."

She tightened his elbows against his side in a defensive gesture. "I didn't mean to, I swear," he said, still chuckling between the words.

Maggie appeared at the back of the truck, and Heidi slipped from the cab and slammed the door. She tossed a still-jovial Frank a glare as she went to help her sister.

"We can get that," Frank said, joining them at the tailgate. "You must be Maggie."

"Uh-huh." Maggie stared up at him, utterly transfixed. Heidi remembered the woozy feeling she'd experienced the first time she'd laid eyes on Frank, and she threw a swift elbow into her sister's arm. Maggie jolted and a hint of redness inched into her face.

"I left Chase in the barn," Frank said. "You're welcome to go see him." He pointed to the dark red structure two buildings down the row. "Through there."

Maggie's face lit up, and she exchanged a glance with Heidi before she left. Heidi reached for a box, a bit embarrassed that her whole life fit into five boxes and one suitcase. She hadn't known how soon she'd be expected to start cleaning, so she'd packed the essentials for easy access.

"Seriously, we'll get it." Frank nodded toward a small group of cowboys Heidi hadn't noticed, and they descended on the truck. "Come with me." His hand flinched toward hers, and he glued it to his side, his jaw tightening.

A smile sprang to her face. Did he want to hold her hand? She wanted to hold his, but she squashed the urge at the sound of multiple footsteps behind hers.

"You're in cabin one," he said as they made their way down the row of trucks toward an expansive lawn in dire need of a trim. The white house sitting in the middle of the grass could use new paint, and new shutters, and—

"You're closest to the house," he continued, yanking her attention from the assessment of his home. "Like I said, you've got new appliances and paint." He moved down a gravel path bordering the lawn, and the first cabin came into view.

"How many cabins are there?" she asked.

"Twelve. Two men in each."

"But this one's empty?" She tried to absorb the vastness of the land beyond the cabins, but it felt huge, never-ending, and she suddenly understood what Frank meant when he said the women he'd dated had liked the idea of him more than him.

"I used to live in it," Frank said, catching her eye and holding on. She saw something deeper to Frank she wanted to dive into and explore.

"And now you don't?" The thought of living where he once had made her stomach flip and her heartrate double.

"I moved into the homestead," he said with a note of longing in his voice. "I'm going to rebuild it, and I figured I could live in the mess during construction as easily as anyone else."

"Do you live there alone?" The white house only sat a hundred yards from her front door, and her head swam with the possibility of having Frank so close. Almost too close.

"No, my dad's still out here. He's planning to move into town by the end of the year. He's building a house on some land he owns there. Two of my brothers still live here too, but they'll both go back to school come fall."

"Like me," ghosted between Heidi's lips, and she wasn't sure if Frank heard her and chose to ignore the statement, or if she'd spoken too quietly for him to notice. He moved up the steps, his cowboy boots clomping on the wood.

"That's my rocking chair," he said. "But you can use it if you want."

She ran her hand along the armrest. "You sat out here and rocked?"

"Why is that funny?" He gestured for the cowboys to take her boxes in, and they filed past her. She'd never seen so many cowboy hats up close. Well, maybe at the dance on Friday night.

"I didn't say it was funny."

"You're laughing."

She cut off the little giggle trickling from her mouth. "I mean, you said you were old, but I didn't realize you'd already graduated to a rocking chair."

He bumped it out of her reach. "I'll take it back to the house when I go."

"No," she said quickly. "I like it. I can watch the—" She glanced over her shoulder to see the view from her front porch. "The—whatever's in that building."

"That's our cow-calf pen," he said.

"Cow-calf?"

"The newborn calves. They don't go out on the range until they're older. Those cows need to be bottle fed."

"And you do that?"

"I do whatever needs to be done." He cleared his throat. "And for the record, I used to sit out here at night and play my guitar. I found it…relaxing." He moved into the house, indicating she come with him.

She stepped into the cabin and took in the light brown walls, the hardwood floors, the small but brand-new kitchen. The living room spread before her, and it housed a couch, a coffee table, and a radio. The kitchen had an eat-in table with two chairs and bright yellow countertops. Two doors stood at the back of the room.

"Bedroom and bathroom?" she asked, pointing to the doors.

"Thanks, guys," Frank said as the cowboys set her boxes on the couch. "Go see where Terry wants you."

They nodded and left, almost like robots.

"I guess you really are the boss," she said.

He turned toward her. "You didn't believe me?"

"I did." She hooked her thumb over her shoulder. "If you left the chair here, what do you do to relax now?"

Alone together, he moved closer to her, puncturing her personal bubble and still advancing. His fingertips brushed against hers. "I don't have time to relax now." His voice came out husky and hoarse, and Heidi swallowed at the desire she heard hiding between the syllables. He held her gaze for one, two, three breaths before stepping past her and exiting. "Oh, and yes, those two doors lead to your bedroom and then the bathroom. I'll let you get settled." He started to pull the door closed, and panic paraded through her with sharp heels.

"Wait." Maybe her voice came out a little screechy. She tried to tame it back into normalcy. "When do you want me to start cleaning?"

He waved his hand like her job meant nothing. "Tomorrow. You get unpacked and settled in. Then come over to the administration trailer, and we'll get your paperwork done." Again, he turned to leave.

"Frank?"

With well-practiced patience, he turned back, his expression curious and open.

"Where's the administration trailer?"

He grinned. "How about I come check on you in about an hour?" He glanced into the sky like he measured time with the sun. Maybe a rancher like him did. "I'll show you around the ranch."

"Okay."

"Okay," he repeated. Then he pulled the door closed and sealed her inside the cabin where he used to live. He seemed to be everywhere out here, and Heidi wondered if moving to the ranch was the right thing.

"Of course it is," she told herself firmly, stepping toward the first box. She'd already felt that affirmation, and she wasn't going to start doubting now.

Frank stood on the front porch, his smile seemingly permanent no matter how he tried to erase it. Because he'd just heard Heidi talk out loud to herself. He wasn't sure why she'd needed to reassure herself with "Of course it is," but this little quirk of hers embedded her deeper into his heart.

And he'd have to be blind not to see the emotions she wore on her face. And he wasn't blind. He'd seen her apprehension, even though she hid it well beneath a wall of determination and strength. He admired that in a woman. Anything was better than a clingy, giggly woman, who laughed at everything he said and pressed into him at every opportunity.

Heidi had also broadcast some definite interest in him, and he hadn't been able to help himself once all the boys had left him alone with her. He wanted to be close to her, and he'd needed to know if she'd let him. And she had.

Something banged in the cabin behind him, startling him into action and down the stairs. He didn't want to be caught on her front porch, fantasizing about things that hadn't happened yet.

He headed over to the brand-new administration building, whistling for Daisy and Duke to join him as he passed the horse barn. They used to live with him in the cabin, but when he'd moved to the homestead, they'd moved to the tack room. Something about the homestead unsettled them, and he missed their calming presence.

A border collie and an Australian shepherd, both dogs earned their keep on the ranch. "Hey, girl." He scrubbed Daisy's black-and-white coat while Duke licked his other hand. He had a happy face, and his colors for a black tricolor shepherd could've won dog shows. Frank had the papers from the American Kennel Club to prove it.

"How's the paw, Duke?" Frank lifted the shepherd's back paw to examine where he'd stepped on a nail last week. "Looks good, bud." He combed his fingers through the dog's copper markings, affection flowing from him. "We got a new lady out here on the ranch. I'll bring her by to meet you guys later, okay? You have to be nice to her."

Daisy and Duke simply cocked their heads and looked at him. "Oh, go on then. Go find Rusty."

Daisy barked, and both dogs ran back into the barn. Rusty ran the horse barn, and he'd keep the dogs company while Frank worked behind the desk. He continued to the administration trailer, an image of Heidi still stuck in his mind. She'd worn jeans out to the ranch today, a smart choice. The bright polka-dot shirt had been a bit disappointing, but Frank supposed she couldn't wear off-the-shoulder sweaters *every* day. Even though he wanted her to.

"Mornin', Boss," Terry said after Frank entered the building and the door crashed closed.

The general controller sat at his desk, and he lifted a manila folder toward Frank. "The paperwork for Miss Duffin."

"Thanks, Terry." Frank took the folder and headed toward the office in the corner of the trailer. It had once been his father's, and the smell of leather and his dad's aftershave still lingered in the air. Frank felt small and insignificant in the space, as he often had as a child. Even when he outgrew his father by three inches, the man still seemed to tower over him. He knew so much about the ranch, and cattle, and taking care of his men, that often Frank felt overwhelmed by the sheer number of tasks to complete in one day.

An hour later, he smelled chocolate and sugar as he walked toward cabin one. The scent made his mouth water as he climbed the steps and knocked on Heidi's door.

She opened it several seconds later, a plate of cookies in her hand and a grin the size of Texas itself on her face. "Want to be my taste-tester?"

He glanced at the cookies, wondering if she'd eaten one yet and he could taste it on her lips. "Is there somethin' wrong with these?"

She shrugged as she painted the air with her light laugh. "I don't know. I made up the recipe, and I want to see if it works."

"It looks like it worked." He swallowed as his mouth continued to water.

"Looks can be deceiving," he said.

"You got that right." He reached for a cookie. "Well, I'll be brave, I guess." He bit into the cookie, expecting a mouthful of salt or something, but it tasted just fine. More than fine. Delicious. "This is fantastic," he said after he swallowed.

"Really?"

He inched forward until she stepped back and let him into the cabin. "Really." He finished the first cookie and reached for another one. "I'll be your taste-tester any time you want." He polished off the second cookie and licked his fingers. He caught her staring at his mouth, and a grin pulled at the corners. "You ready for the ranch tour?"

She startled like she'd forgotten he was there and hurried into the kitchen. He expected it to look like a bomb had gone off, but barely a spoon sat out of place. The only evidence that she'd baked was the empty tray on the stovetop. A quick glance confirmed that the boxes had all been unpacked too.

Frank reached for her hand as she approached him. He smiled at her, pleased and excited when she squeezed his fingers. "I'm really glad you took this job," he murmured, wondering if it was too early in their relationship to kiss her.

It felt like it, and propriety demanded that he release her hand and back up. He didn't need his cowhands gossiping about "the boss's new girlfriend." He probably shouldn't be alone with her in her cabin, either, and so, reluctantly, he let go of her hand and put the required distance between them.

"So, let's start at my place," he said. "I'd love a woman's opinion on how I should rebuild the homestead."

He led her across the yard, the heat of the day already close to unbearable. "So I'm going to hire a gardener this summer too. Dad used to love workin' in the yard, but well—" He cut a glance in her direction to judge her reaction. She seemed open, innocent, non-judgmental. "He's not as young as he used to be."

She nodded. "I understand that. I cleaned my father's storeroom last week, and let's just say it hadn't been done in at least a year. He used to never allow that." She peered around the lawn. "You have a lot of land here. Are you going to expand the homestead? You know, to raise your family here?"

He squinted like he'd never thought of that. "Yeah, probably."

"So you want a family." She wasn't really asking.

"Someday," he said in a non-committal way. "My momma would hit me upside the head if she heard me say that." He chuckled. "She loved us boys, but she told me hundreds of times, 'Frankie, get married and give me some grandgirls.' Of course, I was much too young to get married at the time."

"When did she pass away?" Heidi's question coming from anyone else would've drove annoyance right through his skull. But the delicate way she asked, the way she wanted to help him, understand him, only fanned the flames of attraction burning in his core.

"Almost ten years ago now."

"Was she ill?"

"Yes," Frank whispered. "Breast cancer. They didn't have the tests we have now. At least, she didn't know about them here, and by the time she did, it was too late anyway."

Heidi's hand landed on his arm. Strong and confident, but also light and hesitant. "I'm sorry, Frank."

He slowed his step and gazed at the house. "Me too. I miss her."

"I'm sure you do."

"This place.... It needs to be rebuilt. It needs to find a heart again. Since momma died, it's just been a house." He looked at Heidi, almost desperate to make her understand. "I want to make it a home again."

Her smile came quick and sure, though the sadness still touched her eyes. "You will."

He straightened, the words he wanted to say buried deep. He knew this house needed a good woman to make it a home. Someone who could bring people together—his brothers, his father, all the cowhands—and make them feel part of something bigger than them. Make them feel like they belonged to this ranch, and the ranch belonged to them. Make them all into a family again.

His mother had done that, and as he stood on the lawn with Heidi Duffin, he wondered if she could too.

"Will you help me?" he asked. "I don't have a woman's eye. Maybe you can tell me where things should go, and what I should do."

"I don't know, Frank." She took a step back. "I know how to bake, but I don't know anything about interior design."

"Well, then, let's start with the kitchen." He squared his shoulders and moved toward the back door, which opened into a small mudroom where everyone left their boots, and then continued into the narrow kitchen.

Heidi gasped when she saw it. "Oh, okay. I can help with this."

"It's terrible, isn't it?"

She edged sideways, her hands splayed out to her sides. "How do you even move in here?"

"It's not *that* bad."

"Frankie," she said, a tease in her voice that he adored. "If you want a woman to be happy with this house, it starts in the kitchen. So get in here and make this thing at least five times this big."

Frank threw his head back and laughed. Laughed because Heidi was the most perfect creature he'd ever met. Laughed because she'd taken something of his mother's that had been precious to him and made it alive again. Laughed because part of him was freaking out at how quickly he was falling for this girl who was leaving at the end of the summer.

Chapter Four

Heidi spent the day with Frank, going through his house. Before they'd left the smallest, narrowest kitchen Heidi had ever stepped foot into, he'd grabbed a paper and a pen and taken notes.

As they passed a room on the upper level, she spied a sewing machine. "Frank." She put her hand on his arm to get him to stop, quickly removing it when electricity jumped from him to her. Or maybe from her to him. She wasn't sure.

"Tell me about that sewing machine."

He leaned into the doorway with her. "That was my mother's."

Hope flared through Heidi, but her request seemed to stick in her throat. But surely she could buy fabric in this town, small as it was. And she did love to put pieces together….

"Would you mind—?" she asked at the same time Frank said, "Want me to bring it over to your place?"

A nervous giggle escaped her mouth, followed by a long exhale. "I'd love that," she said, beaming up at him. "If it's okay."

"'Course it's okay." He cast a long look back at the sewing machine. "Momma would want someone to use it."

They'd finished walking through the house, and now, they

wandered down the dirt road that led to his homestead, the evening sun as hot as ever. "You better not do everything I said," she said.

"Why not?" He scuffed his boots in the dirt, his hands tucked safely in his pockets. "I liked what you had to say about the house. It just affirmed everything I've been feeling about it."

"It's not my house," she said, keeping an eye on him for his reaction.

He gave her none, which annoyed her. Frank was very, very good at keeping a mask of nonchalance in place. It seemed nothing ruffled his feathers. "I may not do everything you said," he said. "But your suggestions were good. I love the idea of a deck off the kitchen."

"You'll have to re-landscape the whole yard."

"Yep."

"Oh, but you have the money for that."

That brought his eyes to hers. "Ranching is a lot of work," he said, his voice even and deep and as wonderful as the first time she'd met him. "But I spend a lot of time in my office now that I'm the boss. Landscaping and building the house will be good for me."

She wasn't sure why she'd snapped at him. Her irritation faded, and she stepped closer to him, slipping her hand into the crook of his elbow. "So, is that how you'll relax in the evenings this summer?"

"Probably."

Not the answer she wanted. Though he hadn't objected to her touch, he hadn't exactly returned it either. *What do you want him to say?* she wondered as the country silence smothered her.

She knew. She wanted him to say he'd come by her place and they'd relax on her front porch together. That he'd bring his guitar and sing for her in that intoxicating voice. That he'd hold her hand as they watched the stars wink into existence.

"You want to eat dinner with us tonight?" he asked. "I don't think there's much in that cabin."

"I found enough to make cookies."

"You eat cookies for dinner?"

She smiled and sighed. "Not usually, unfortunately."

He pressed his elbow against his side, a squeeze on her hand, but he didn't speak.

"I should probably go into town and get groceries. Then I'll be ready for the week." She still hadn't signed anything to start work. "I want to start cleaning tomorrow."

His footsteps slowed, and he turned toward her, shielding her from the setting sun. He gazed down on her, and she thought a kiss with him at twilight would be the most wonderful thing in the world. She tilted her head up to meet his eyes, but her gaze lingered on his mouth.

"Would you mind if I came with you?"

"To go grocery shopping?"

"Well, maybe not that part." The corners of his mouth kicked up. He held her eyes, his hands sliding out of his pockets and taking hers. "Maybe you'd let me take you to dinner."

Heidi didn't see how anything good could come from going to dinner with him. She already felt overwhelmed with desire for him, and yet, in the back of her mind, she knew she couldn't have him. He belonged here in Three Rivers, and she…well, she didn't.

He threaded his fingers between hers while he waited for her answer. "Just friends," he murmured.

"You hold all your friends' hands?" she asked, her voice breathless and weak among all this sky, all this land, Frank's huge presence.

"No." He leaned down and the tip of his hat bumped against the top of her head as his lips touched her temple. "I like you, Heidi."

Fear raced through her with the speed of a freight train. She liked him too. Too much already.

"Do you like me?"

She usually liked a man who didn't play games. Westin had thrown so many wild cards her way, she'd never known how he felt, what he was thinking. She much preferred Frank's straightforward nature.

"Yes," she whispered.

"Then dinner would be fine," he pressed.

She looked up at him, found his eyes only inches from hers, and his mouth tilted slightly farther away than that. "I'm going back to school in September."

"That's just fine."

"It is?" Heidi hated that the words came out of her mouth, but she couldn't suck them back in.

Frank stepped back and drew a deep breath into his broad chest. "I won't ask you to stay when it's time to go." He turned his head and looked toward the homestead. "But I won't lie and say I'm not interested in you."

Heidi's heart swelled and warmed with his words. She'd never felt this way about anyone before, not that she'd given herself much of a chance. Everyone in Amarillo had known she was leaving, and no one had seemed that interested in persuading her to stay. And in San Francisco, she'd dated Westin for the first six months, had her heart stomped on, and given up the idea of dating in favor of focusing on her baking.

Frank presented a whole new hurdle she'd never experienced before.

"Dinner, then," she said, making her voice light. "I like talking to you, Frank, and I'm...interested in knowing more about you."

His electric eyes came back to her face, and they burned, and branded, and bored straight into her. He smiled, and weakness spread through Heidi. For the first time in over a decade, she wondered if culinary school was the right thing to do.

Confusion cascaded through her, and she faced her cabin. "Let me grab my purse."

"I'll get my keys. My truck's in the garage. Come on over to the homestead when you're ready to go."

She nodded and strode away from him. Though evening had come, several cowhands continued to work around the barn and animal buildings. They lifted their hands in friendly waves as she moved down the gravel path to her cabin, and she returned their gestures. But inside, she felt like running, and running fast.

She made it inside her cabin and closed the door. She twisted the lock hard and pressed her back against the door, her chest heaving with panic.

Calm down, calm down, *she told herself.* Its just dinner.

But Heidi knew her panic attack had been brought on by more than dinner. It had been triggered by the very idea of abandoning her lifelong dreams of owning a bakery.

As she coached herself to take deep breaths and think rationally, she wondered if Frank would be worth giving up everything she'd worked for so long to achieve.

She squared her shoulders. He'd just said he wouldn't ask her to stay when it was time for her to leave. She didn't know everything about Frank Ackerman, but she had learned that he was a man of honor. She believed him when he said he wouldn't ask her to stay.

Calmed, Heidi checked her makeup and hair, touching up the imperfections brought on by her anxiety and the heat, collected her purse, and made her way over to the homestead.

The next morning, Heidi woke in a strange place. Several roosters crowed, almost in unison, and she remembered she'd moved to Three Rivers Ranch.

A slow grin painted her face as she remembered the previous night's dinner. Frank had been nothing but a gentleman, paying for their Italian feast before taking her on a tour of downtown Three Rivers.

True to his word, he waited in the truck while she picked out fabric and then grocery shopped, an event prolonged by everyone's interest in the new woman in town. They'd been nice, but curious, and more than one had shown their surprise at her living out at the ranch. Apparently, women didn't normally do that.

Heidi didn't care. Women didn't normally go to culinary school in San Francisco either. Heidi had always done what she felt was right for her, even if society wasn't quite ready for it yet.

She pushed her blankets back and got out of bed just as a knock sounded on her door. A shock traveled through her and she looked down at her pajamas. Fully covered, she decided she could crack the door and get rid of whoever stood there.

"Mornin'," Frank said when she opened the door four inches. She kept as much of her body behind it as possible.

"You're up early," she said.

He chuckled. "The curse of a rancher." He scanned what little of her he could see through the crack. "I can see I'm too early for you." He fell back two steps. "Just wanted to stop by and let you know to come on over to the admin trailer this morning. You can meet everyone and then get started."

"How long do I have?"

"I'd say about twenty minutes." He beamed at her and rocked on his heels.

"You're enjoying yourself too much," she said. "You could've mentioned what time I needed to be ready to me last night."

"I could've." Frank's smile widened. "But then I wouldn't have had this chance to talk to you."

"Get out of here." She added a laugh to her playful tone and closed the door. Twenty minutes. It would take that long to get her heart to settle down from Frank's flirtations.

Nineteen minutes later, she climbed the grated steps to the administration trailer. He'd shown it to her yesterday, as well as the supply closet where she'd find her cleaning supplies. She braced herself to enter the building. Yesterday, it had been empty except for one man—Terry, the general controller.

But Frank had said, "meet everyone," and her heart thundered now for an entirely different reason.

"You've got this," she said to herself. "They can't fire you." She pushed into the building in time to hear Frank say, "Okay, guys, let's get started." He glanced up as the door crashed closed behind her, a smile brightening his entire person.

She slipped down the aisle and joined the group on the fringes. But Frank wouldn't let her stay there. He called her to his side and introduced her to the swarm of cowboys. They said hello non-verbally with lifted hands and nods, and Heidi wasn't quite sure how to reciprocate.

"Hello," she said, the way a normal person greeted another. She found Chase's friendly face in the crowd, and smiled at him.

"She'll be doing three cabins each day," he said. "And the administration building and parts of the horse barns on the other days." He glanced at her, as this was new information for her. She took it in stride and kept her arms folded across her chest. "She doesn't do laundry, and she'd not your personal maid. She's here to vacuum and mop and clean bathrooms. If she can't see your floor, she won't vacuum it. Fair?"

Murmurs of assent passed through the crowd. Heidi liked this powerful, in-charge side of Frank. He didn't speak loud, or aggressively. But everyone in the room knew who steered the ship, including Heidi.

"Good, I'll let Terry give out the assignments for today." Frank stepped away from a big chalkboard and caught Heidi's eye as he ducked around the corner. She didn't need to be standing in front of two dozen men, so she followed him. She watched him disappear into the corner office, and she moved back toward the exit, where the supply closet housed her cleaning items. She got what she needed and headed back toward her place.

"Cabins two, three, and four," she recited to herself. She wasn't sure how long it would take to do each cabin, but she'd soon find out. A ring of keys had been clipped in the three-ring binder, which also detailed each of her chores and who lived in which cabin.

She located the key for cabin two and climbed the steps. After unlocking the door and entering, Heidi wasn't sure if she'd thought through the job. The smell of man and horse and dirty socks almost overwhelmed her.

Taking a steeling breath, she dragged the vacuum into the cabin behind her and got to work. At least she'd have something interesting to tell Maggie that night.

Frank had to work hard to keep himself behind the desk when he knew Heidi was only yards away, cleaning. But he wasn't sure who'd seen them walking together last night, or if anyone had watched them leave together.

He wasn't sure why he cared. Most of the cowhands knew he'd

accelerated his dating, and though only his closest friends had asked why, the reason had to be obvious. And when he started knocking out walls and re-forming the yard, everyone would know he was thinking long-term, looking ahead to a wife and a family.

Frank wasn't sure if he should be embarrassed about that or not. It didn't feel like something he should be self-conscious about, but well, he still felt that way.

And so he confined himself to his office, startling every time the door slammed closed. He'd learned to ignore it over the months, but today, it grabbed his attention every time. Because maybe it was Heidi, returning from her tasks. Maybe she'd pop her head in to see him, to say hello, something.

As the day wore on, and she didn't come, Frank's mood darkened. Almost near quitting time, the door closed, but his hopes didn't lift. She wasn't coming, and he'd been thinking for the past hour of how he could stop by her place without being too obvious.

Then he wondered why he needed to worry about being obvious. He'd flat-out told her last night that he liked her, was interested in her.

She'd taken it well, though pure horror had flowed through him at his boldness. Heidi already knew more about Frank than any of the women he'd dated in the past several months.

"Hey, there."

He jerked his eyes from the report he'd been reading about the price of hay to find Heidi framed in his doorway. She carried something in a paper sack, and it smelled like heaven.

He leaned back in his chair, pure delight pouring through him at the sight of her wearing a pair of jeans and a blue blouse with frilly sleeves under an apron. "You baked?"

She grinned as she bounced into his office. "Well, I had an hour for lunch, so I made the bread dough then. It rose while I finished the last cabin, and it baked while I showered. So...yeah, I baked." She set the paper bag on his desk.

He reached for it, surprised and pleased when he found the loaf of bread still warm. "Heidi, you're...somethin' special." He opened the bag and inhaled the beautiful aroma of freshly baked bread. "I need butter and jam for this. Come on." He stood, completely abandoning the rest of his work—it would be there tomorrow anyway—and hooked his head toward the exit.

She came with him, and they walked side-by-side back to the homestead. She told him about the cleaning, and he simply basked in the sound and beauty of her voice, her personality, her life.

You're in so much trouble, he thought as he opened the back door of the house and ushered her inside. He'd promised her he wouldn't ask her to stay when it came time for her to leave, but he regretted saying so after only one day. What would his heart be like come September? Could he survive her walking away from him then?

Better to end things now, he thought, but the very idea had his intestines in knots and his heart withering into a stone. It had been hard to tell her he owned Three Rivers Ranch. Saying good-bye to her would be impossible.

He came back to reality as she opened and closed drawers, muttering, "knife, knife." He opened the lazy Susan and pulled out the knife block, but Heidi looked at it like he'd just produced a slime ball.

She met his eye and recovered quickly, pulling out a serrated knife and slicing into her bread. "Do you like the end?"

"Not if you do." He liked her, everything about her, from watching her work to being near her. Everything in him calmed when he was with her, and he'd never felt like that before.

"Frank."

"No, I want a middle piece." He turned away from her, from his insane desires, and pulled from the fridge a stick of butter and a jar of apricot preserves.

She was smiling when he set the condiments on the counter beside her. "What?"

"Nothing." She glanced at the butter. "Do you have a microwave oven?"

"Yes." Relief flowed through him that he could say they did. "Should I soften this?"

"I would."

He put the butter on a plate and stuck it in the microwave, then stared helplessly at the buttons.

"Let me." She nudged him out of the way, but he didn't go far. Certainly not far enough to be appropriate, but Heidi didn't seem to mind. "Honestly, how do you men survive over here?"

"It's really hard," he said. "We mostly grill hamburgers or hot dogs and eat sandwiches. My dad makes oatmeal every day, though."

"Oatmeal?" She pulled the butter from the microwave. "Did he make that jam too?"

"No, Miss Frannie gave us that. She was my mother's best friend." A wave of missing hit Frank. Not only for his mother, but for her friends too. They used to come out to the ranch at Christmastime, for barbeques in the summer, to can copious amounts of peaches and tomatoes and spaghetti sauces, to celebrate their children's birthday parties.

"I can't wait to try it." Heidi gave him a raised-eyebrow look, buttered her end piece of bread, and slathered some of the preserves on it. He watched her, transfixed, as she bit into it and licked her lips. The temperature in the kitchen rose at least twenty degrees, and Frank hadn't even eaten yet.

Heidi moaned, chewed, and swallowed. "That jam is divine." She glanced at her handiwork. "And my bread is pretty fantastic too." She looked at him from boots to the top of his hat. "You're not going to try it?" She cocked one hip. "You said you'd be my taste-tester."

Frank flew into action, spreading butter and then jam on the most perfectly brown wheat bread he'd ever seen. Sure enough, when he tasted it, the flavor transported his taste buds to an entirely different plane.

"Holy cow, Heidi." He sagged against the counter. "That's fantastic."

She glowed under the weight of his compliment, but accepted it graciously and took another bite of her bread. Frank wondered why no one in San Francisco had snatched her up. A woman who looked like her and could bake too? Frank felt like he'd won the lottery, and he had to remind himself that Heidi was not his.

Not yet, anyway.

He finished his bread and reached for the knife. Heidi placed her hand on his. "I threw a quick chili together. Maybe you'd like to come have another piece of bread with that?" The hope she wore in her eyes was unmistakable, and joy crashed over Frank that this energy he felt between them was two-sided.

"Sure, but chili? Isn't it kinda hot for soup?"

She gaped at him. "Soup is a year-round dish."

He laughed. "Okay, Miss Heidi. Let's go."

"Bring that jam," she said over her shoulder as she squeezed behind him in the narrow kitchen.

"I'm gonna grab the sewing machine too." Frank disappeared down the hallway and stalled in the doorway to the spare bedroom where the sewing machine sat. A keen sense of nostalgia washed over him, and he pictured his mother bent over the machine, working fabric into something beautiful. He could almost hear the whir of the machine, smell his mother's perfume, feel the fabric of the shirt she'd made for him last.

"You don't have to let me use it." Heidi's soft voice punctured his memories, and he startled.

"No," he said quickly. "No, its fine." He flew into action, unplugging the machine and wrapping it up for the trip across the lawn. They made their way back to her place, and Frank went inside and placed the sewing machine on her kitchen table.

"I'll wait out here." He quickly went back outside while she began to dish up two bowls of chili. She returned a few minutes later with two bowls, along with the bread, butter, and jam on a platter. She settled next to him on the top step and set the platter of food between them.

"How'd you learn how to cook?" he asked. "I mean, besides the baking. I'm assuming they don't teach chili recipes in pastry school."

She smiled and took a bite of her chili. "They don't."

"Hey."

Frank glanced up to see Chase and another cowboy, Matty, at the bottom of Heidi's stairs.

"Evenin', boys."

"That smells delicious." Chase grinned at Heidi. "Maggie said you were a great cook."

"You want some?"

"Yes," both men said together, and Frank scooted over to make room for them as Heidi bounded back into the cabin. "Try the bread," he told them. "It'll change your life."

Matty sliced the bread and they doctored it up with the condiments before Heidi returned. When she did, Chase said, "This is the best bread I've ever had."

"Don't tell my sister that," she said with a smile. "In fact, don't tell her you ate here tonight."

"Why not?"

Heidi shot a look at Frank, but he couldn't interpret it. "She thinks I might steal you away," Heidi finally said. She giggled. "Ridiculous, right?"

"I don't know," Matty said. "I know what Chase usually eats, and this is ten times better."

"Hey," Chase protested. "I don't see you makin' anything better."

Matty laughed. "He's right. I can barely make toast."

Frank laughed with the other men, but he kept his eye on Heidi. She watched them all eating her food, her fingers nervously gripping her spoon and she didn't take another bite of her chili.

"It's great, Heidi," he said. "Really great." He finished eating, set his bowl to the side, and leaned back on his palms. "Nice night, isn't it, boys?"

"Real nice," Chase agreed. Matty's mouth was stuffed too full to answer, so he just nodded. Heidi seemed to have lost her ability to speak.

"Well, I have to go start tearing apart the homestead," he said, already tired as he stood. "I'll see you all tomorrow." He forced himself to move down the steps as the others said good-night, forced himself to walk away from Heidi without looking back. He knew Matty and Chase didn't present a threat when it came to her, but he wanted to spend all his free time with her.

But the fact was, he didn't have free time. Not if he wanted to rebuild the homestead before the winter rains came.

Not if he wanted to have a home that would convince city-girl Heidi Duffin to become his country girl.

By the end of the week, he'd completely gutted the house. TJ and Ben had been on-board to help him, and the three of them working in the evenings had made a big job manageable.

"Now what?" Ben asked as he leaned against the side of a Dumpster Frank had parked next to the garage. It was almost full, and he'd need to call and get it emptied next week.

"Now we add-on," he said, moving around the house to the side that faced the ranch buildings. "I'm going to push the upstairs out over this hill, which I'm going to excavate so we can have a patio down here." He gestured to the land where the patio would be. "There will be a deck above the patio, and that will lead into a kitchen that's five times as big as what we've got now."

"We'll be able to walk out of the basement?" TJ asked.

"Yeah," Frank said. "I'm having Vince come out on Monday. He's going to get the existing lawn in shape and give me advice about the reshaping of everything." He exhaled, more exhausted than he'd been in months.

"You've gone soft since sittin' behind that desk." Ben slapped Frank's bicep in a joking, brotherly gesture.

"That's hard in it's own way," Frank said. "But it's not haulin' hay and branding cows and wrestling cattle through gates, that's for sure."

"Let's go out on the range this weekend," TJ said suddenly. "Just the three of us, like we used to as kids."

"Miles would come when we were kids," Frank said softly, a hole opening in his heart for his baby brother that he hadn't realized existed.

Ben's usual joviality had faded, and he watched Frank, who always bore the burden of being the oldest. "Maybe I'll call him tonight," Frank said. "And we can go in the morning." He tossed a look toward cabin one, where Heidi had sat for the past several nights, rocking in his chair and reading while he and his brothers tore their house apart.

TJ grinned and followed Frank's gaze. "And you can tell us about your new girlfriend."

Franks insides seized and he pulled his gaze from her cabin. "She's not my girlfriend."

"But you like her," TJ pressed.

Frank had already told her that, and he trusted his brothers. With a sigh, he said, "Yeah, too much." He lifted the shovel he'd carried around the house and drove it into the ground. "She's leavin' the same time you two are." He met each of their eyes for a brief moment. "A weekend away will be good for me."

TJ nodded and moved toward the backdoor. "I'll get the gear ready."

Ben stayed with Frank, but Frank didn't appreciate the weight of his brother's stare. "Spit it out, Ben."

"If you don't want to go, it's okay."

"I do want to go." But Frank couldn't stop himself from looking at cabin one. What about Heidi was so magnetic? Why did he feel this inexplicable need to be near her?

"We'll miss church."

"I've missed church before." Loads of times, actually. The life of a rancher never ended, not even on the Sabbath. He'd worked out a system where he could go, though, and he relied on his less religious cowhands to do the morning chores on Sundays. Dad had always done only the necessary tasks of feeding and watering animals on Sunday, something Frank planned to continue.

"Frank—"

He trained his eyes on his brother. "I'm fine, Ben. We need to go for TJ. He's had a rough couple of years." Frank wasn't entirely sure why, but if TJ wanted to spend time with him and Ben, that was a good sign. "Maybe he'll tell us what's going on with him."

"Maybe," Ben said, but he didn't sound as hopeful as Frank felt. "I'm gonna go call Rebecca and tell her I'll be gone for the weekend."

"I'll get the food ready and check with Rusty about takin' the horses."

Ben nodded and left Frank standing in the dusky night. He could pack their food in the morning, so he headed over to the horse barn to see if Rusty was still there. He should've gone home a while ago, and Frank hoped he had so he could be alone for a few minutes with the horses.

He wandered down the middle aisle, noticing the hard work that went into keeping the barn clean and the horses fed and happy. With a whistle, Daisy and Duke popped their heads out of the tack room. They bounded toward him, their tails wagging like flags.

He crouched down and rubbed his hands over their heads and ears. "Hey, guys. Hey." He chuckled as they licked his wrists and arms, a sense of peace and contentment filtering through him despite his exhaustion, his worries, his problems.

He knew he needed to get away from the ranch for a while, and he couldn't wait until tomorrow. "Let's go for a ride. You want to?" He turned and headed toward the parking lot. After a quick stop into the house to let Ben know where he was going, Frank loaded up his dogs in the back of his truck, and drove.

He'd never been able to get away from the things plaguing him by driving, but he'd always been able to get the kinks in his mind worked out. He just hoped that would be true this time too, because he honestly didn't know what to do about Heidi.

He knew he didn't want to get his heart broken come September when she left. But his heart felt like shattered glass when he thought of only being friends with her. He returned to the ranch two hours later, still just as knotted and confused as when he'd left.

Chapter Five

Heidi spent Saturday in the administration building, wiping walls and windows, vacuuming, and emptying garbage cans. The cowhands also had a little kitchenette, and she cleaned the counters, the sink, and inside the microwave.

Terry had warned her against opening the fridge before he'd left for lunch. He said they ran a skeleton crew on the weekends, and he took the morning shift so others could sleep in on Saturdays or go to church on Sundays.

And that had gotten Heidi thinking about church. She'd normally go with her family, and she wanted to keep attending here. Snakes writhed in her chest whenever she thought about making the drive on her own—which she'd never done—and sitting in a pew by herself. She hadn't given it much thought, but she supposed she would've sat with Frank at church.

But he'd gone out on the range early-early Saturday morning. He'd stopped by late on Friday night to tell her, looking worn at the edges and exhausted through and through. She'd wanted to send him with something to eat, but she hadn't had time to make anything.

She missed his presence on the ranch. It was strange how everything felt different without him here, almost like the magical quality of the ranch actually belonged to Frank and not the land. Heidi had definitely felt different out here than she had in Amarillo or San Francisco. She felt more like who she truly was, not like she was trying to fit into a mold someone thought she should.

Which made no sense. She'd never felt pressured to do anything she didn't want to do. Pastry school had been her choice, and it was an expensive and difficult experience.

As she finished cleaning the admin building and put her supplies away, she realized that out here, she didn't have to be or do anything other than what she already was and did. Life in the country really was easier, because it was simpler.

"Doesn't mean I'm a country girl," she muttered as she left the building and returned to her cabin. With only half the day gone, and nothing to occupy her time until church the next morning, she pulled out her favorite cookbook and settled on her bed to read. She would've sat in Frank's rocking chair, but the mid-day heat knocked the breath from her lungs. Only the second week of June, this summer promised to be a scorcher.

Her nerves stayed with her through the afternoon and into the evening. Someone knocked on the door just before six, and Heidi half-hoped it would be Frank, back from the range. A ridiculous thought, because he'd told her he wouldn't be back until Sunday evening.

Chase stood on the front porch, his fingers clutching a square folding table. "I found one, Miss Heidi."

A smile bloomed on her face. "Set it up right there on the porch, Chase. I'll get the pulled pork." She'd been feeding Chase every night since Tuesday, and he often brought a few other cowboys with him. Heidi found she enjoyed their company, especially since Frank kept his head buried in ranch work during the day and renovations at night. He hadn't stopped by once, but Heidi hadn't expected him to. Not really.

Sure, her heart longed for him to join his cowhands at her cabin for dinner. But she understood why he didn't. Or at least she told herself she understood.

"I invited everyone tonight," he said as she brought out her slow cooker full of meat. "Let me get that, Miss Heidi."

She passed the heavy appliance to him and he set it on the end of the table. "I'll get the buns and coleslaw. Anyone is invited, Chase."

He beamed at her and she returned to the house for the rest of the meal. She paused and looked out the window that faced the range, sending a silent prayer that Frank would know he was missed at this dinner.

Keep him safe, she prayed. Then she went out to the porch, where Matty, Terry, and a young cowboy no older than twenty named Cash had already shown up.

"Evenin', boys," she drawled like a real cowgirl. A smile slipped over her face and she giggled. "You can eat after we say grace."

Chase said it, and Heidi made a mental note to tell Maggie how wonderful he was. They'd seen each other at the town dance again last night, but Heidi hadn't gone. She hadn't wanted to go alone, even though Chase had invited her to go with him and Matty. No, she wanted to go with Frank, but he didn't mention it. In fact, he worked on the house until darkness fell, and then he left in his truck.

Maybe he'd gone to the dance without her. Maybe he had a country girl he kept at the ranch and a town girl he met on the weekends.

Heidi had been horrified by such thoughts, but Victoria's snide remark about being the flavor of the month still echoed loudly in her brain from time to time. And Westin *had* kept another girl in another city. Heidi didn't want to repeat that, not even a little bit.

"Thank you, Miss Heidi." Each cowboy who moved through the line treated her with respect and kindness, and she loaded up her plate and sat on the steps with them, enjoying her time in the evenings with these cowboys.

She shook her head at the stories Terry told about a blizzard in Wyoming, where he grew up, and she laughed when Matty started doing his impressions of Ronald Reagan. Heidi couldn't quite believe these men had wormed their way into her heart after only a week, but they were good men. After they'd left, after she'd cleaned up, after she'd settled down for the night, she wondered exactly when she'd started liking cowboys.

She smiled to herself as she turned onto her side and closed her eyes. The answer was clear. She'd started liking cowboys about the same time she'd splashed red punch down the front of one.

The following morning found Heidi with a hive of bees in her throat. She'd managed to get up and get ready. She'd asked Chase for a ride to church, but he'd pulled the morning chores that Sunday. He'd given her the keys to his truck, and she'd gotten herself to town. Gotten herself all the way to the church, thank you very much. She'd only had to stop once to get directions.

But now she couldn't make herself go in. Mothers and fathers walked past where she sat in the cab, with children skipping around them. Older couples went in together. Single men and women, but Heidi knew none of them would sit alone for long. They had friends and families they knew and could sit with.

She didn't have anyone.

"Just go in," she told herself. "You've done this before. You can do this again." Finding a church in San Francisco hadn't been hard, but going for the first time certainly had. That same swarm of bees had assaulted her then, as it did now. The first few weeks had been rough, but then she'd found friends and made connections. She missed her friends there keenly now. She thought of Jenny and Damon, the two who lived nearest to her and attended the same church. They'd often walk together and go back to one of their apartments for lunch afterward.

No one from her pastry school attended the same church, but she had friends in her classes too. Julie, and Savannah, and Karen. Heidi generally got along just fine with most people, and yet the buzzing in her chest didn't diminish.

She finally worked up enough courage to get out of the truck. The bells rang, and she realized the sermon was about to start without her. Hurrying now, she slipped through the doors and glided across the foyer. The chapel doors were still open, but as soon as she stepped inside, the ushers closed them.

She glanced around, frantic for somewhere to sit. It seemed everyone who attended the dances on Friday nights also came to church. Not a spare seat could be found—at least at the back.

The usher pointed to the left, and she found a pocket of empty space between two elderly couples. Without another choice, Heidi made her way toward the seat. She managed to get to it without embarrassing herself too badly, but surely every single person in the place had seen her.

The pastor didn't break his stride, but Heidi had a hard time listening to him. Instead, she focused on finding her own center and infusing some of the peace permeating the chapel into her heart.

She caught the end of his speech, and he spoke about staying true during difficult times. He promised that hard things would come to each person, and it was only through those trials that they could prove to the Lord—and themselves—who they really were. What they were really made of.

Uplifted, Heidi stood for the closing hymn with everyone else, satisfied with her choice to come to church, even if she'd had to do it by herself. When the meeting ended, people swarmed the aisles. Children who'd been sitting for too long ran, and mothers who hadn't had a long enough break called after them.

"Are you going to the picnic?"

Heidi turned toward the voice to find a woman about her age leaning over the back of the pew two rows up. She pointed to herself, and the woman nodded.

"I hadn't planned on it," Heidi said. Chase hadn't said anything about a picnic.

The woman had long waves of dark hair, bushy bangs, and cinnamon colored eyes that seemed more predatory than kind. "Probably for the best."

Heidi had no idea what that meant, but she didn't sense a friend in the woman. She turned away, hoping to escape before the conversation could continue.

"I heard y'all were livin' out at the ranch," the woman said.

"Yes," Heidi said, disinterested in repeating some of the conversations she'd had at the grocery store.

"Oh, you're the one living at the ranch?" Another woman stopped at the end of Heidi's aisle, blocking her escape. She had red hair that had seen ten too many perms. Her green eyes narrowed at Heidi. "So you're Frank's girlfriend."

She shook her head. "No. I clean—"

"She is."

Heidi swung toward the familiar voice, her stomach dropping and her pulse skyrocketing when she saw Victoria.

"I'm not," Heidi insisted. "I just got a job out there. That's all."

"I just can't believe he's dating someone again," the redhead said, but she wasn't talking to Heidi. The dark-haired woman moved out of her aisle to comfort her.

"It's okay, Claire. Frank's not the only bachelor in town."

"You would know, Whitney." Victoria's acidic tone could apparently apply to everyone, something that made Heidi feel the teensiest bit better.

"So would you, Vickie." Whitney shot Victoria a glare, put her arm around Claire, and they left.

Desperate to escape Victoria, Heidi moved swiftly out of her row, keeping her back to the other woman.

"When will you be leaving town?" Victoria called after her.

Heidi barely turned. "September. That's when I go back to school."

Victoria said something else, but Heidi slipped into the foyer and out into the sunshine before she heard it. She didn't want to hear it. Didn't want more of Victoria's words to loop through her mind in her moments of self-doubt.

She cured her insecurities and erased the damaging conversation by baking. Cookies, a chocolate cake, and a long row of lemon tarts later, Heidi finally felt normal again. But if she consumed even a fraction of what she'd churned out, she'd be sick all night.

So she did what any good neighbor would do: She loaded up some of everything and headed next door. In this case, it was to the homestead. She had no idea if Frank had returned yet, and with every step she told herself it didn't matter. She wanted to meet his brothers face-to-face, not just spy on them from over the top of her book. And she hadn't seen his father once.

She went to the front door and knocked, a sharp, sure knock that wouldn't go unnoticed. A few moments later, an older gentleman answered the door.

"Mister Ackerman." Heidi smiled at him and indicated the treats she carried. "I'm your new housekeeper, Heidi Duffin. I made a few too many goodies, and I thought you'd like some."

He blinked at her, and she saw Frank in him. "Heidi, sure. Frank's talked about ya." He stepped back. "C'mon in. Afraid Frank's not here."

"Oh, I know." Heidi stepped through the door and right into a construction zone. Cardboard covered the bare wood floor, and only the bare necessities for furniture remained—a recliner and a loveseat.

"I brought these for you," she said, glad she'd worn her sneakers. "He told me you have quite the sweet tooth."

"He's tellin' my secrets, is he?" He tacked on a chuckle at the end. "Well, I guess he didn't lie. Let's see what you got."

She followed him into the equally demolished kitchen and set the tray on the counter. "Those are oatmeal chocolate chip cookies." She pointed. "And lemon tarts. And a nice, thick piece of chocolate cake."

"I'll take that." He pulled a spoon from the drawer and opened the fridge. "You mind if I pour a little cream on it? That's how my wife used to serve it."

Heidi beamed at him. "Cream only makes things better."

He peered at her for a moment, a small blip in time, but it felt like he could see everything about her in that brief window. "So you're cleanin' our cabins." He poured a bit of cream over the cake.

"Yes, sir."

He gestured for her to go back into the living room and sit. So she did. He took up his position in the recliner and spooned some cake into his mouth. "This is delicious. You're a great baker, Miss Duffin."

Pride swelled in her chest. "Thank you."

"I don't think my wife's was even this good."

"Well, it's been a long time, sir. I'm sure her cake was delicious."

Again, he looked straight through her, almost like she wasn't there, before taking another bite. "So what brings you to Three Rivers?"

She told him about the job, and her schooling in San Francisco, and her desire to open a bakery.

"I'd buy a chocolate cake from your bakery every week," he said.

"Oh, no one can eat a chocolate cake every week." Heidi laughed, though she secretly hoped they could. It would certainly keep her in business.

"You're probably right. Doc wouldn't like that. He complains about my cholesterol." Frank's father stood and took the dish into the kitchen. "In fact, I don't think I'm gonna tell anyone about that cake." He flashed her a grin.

"It'll be our little secret." Heidi stood. "Well, I've bothered you for long enough. Enjoy the rest another time. Or give them to your boys."

He walked her to the door. "Thank you, Miss Duffin." He gave her a sincere smile, and a pang of sadness hit Heidi right beneath her breastbone. She said good-night, though it wasn't quite dinnertime yet, and hurried back to her cabin. She needed to call her parents and tell them she loved them. Even if her dad had been stubborn and pouty about her coming out here. Even if she sometimes wished she hadn't had to cook dinner and feed her sisters while her mom taught piano.

People weren't perfect, and her parents had tried. They were good people, like the Ackermans. A keen sense of forgiveness washed over her, and a burden Heidi had been carrying alone for a long time vanished. She hoped that one day, when she had kids, they would be able to forgive her for the things she didn't quite do right.

The thoughts of a family startled her. It had always been a bakery first. Family fell way down the line. Always had. But with a backward glance to the homestead, she thought of Frank's father, and Frank, and the obvious love they each held for their mother, even a decade after her death.

And Heidi wanted that kind of love in her life. She ducked inside and picked up the phone.

Frank woke on Sunday morning, hopeful TJ would be as forthcoming today as he had been yesterday. He stepped outside and set a kettle on the portable stove and scooped instant coffee into three mugs. His brothers would be up by the time the water boiled, he knew. The Ackerman men operated on a schedule, even when they rode out on the range.

They'd ridden out to a cabin about an hour from the homestead, where they ate breakfast before continuing further into the wilderness.

Keeping their horses to a slow walk, Frank had been able to talk to his brothers. Really find out how they felt about things. He wasn't worried about Ben, though Ben wasn't quite sure he could be successful in Dallas.

Frank and TJ had assured him he could. They'd talked about Rebecca, and Ben's plans to propose to her by the end of the summer.

"You have a ring?" Frank asked.

"Not yet." Ben kept his eye on the horizon, and Frank understood why. "Dad said he'd give me the money. I need to talk to her father, and I have no idea what kind of ring she'd like."

"Take her with you," TJ suggested. "That's all the rage now. Women selecting their own wedding rings."

"It is?" Frank hadn't known that, but he didn't know much outside the boundaries of the ranch. He could barely operate under the societal rules of Three Rivers, as evidenced by his disastrous dating attempts.

TJ had then confessed that he didn't like engineering. Frank had been shocked, and it had taken several strides of the horse for him to figure out what to say. And even then, all he'd said was, "What are you gonna do about that?"

And that was the problem. TJ didn't know what to do. He was one year away from a degree in engineering, and he didn't want it. Frank had offered for him to stay on at the ranch, but TJ had vetoed it.

"I like ranching," he'd said. "But…don't take this the wrong way, but there aren't any opportunities here."

"Opportunities?"

"Ben can't even open a dental practice."

"He's right," Ben had said. "Three Rivers isn't the place for someone if they don't know what to do with their life."

Frank hadn't known what to think, or what to say. So he prayed, and he waited for inspiration to say what the Lord wanted him to. So he'd spoken very little. Which had turned out okay, because TJ was the one who needed to talk.

"Morning," Ben said as he came out of the remote cabin where they'd stayed the night. He took a deep breath and exhaled. "I love this land."

"Me too." Frank handed him a mug with instant coffee granules already in it. "Water's hot."

"How long you been up?"

"Long enough to boil water."

Ben stepped to the portable stove TJ had packed and poured water into his mug. "So you didn't talk much yesterday."

"Not much to say."

Ben took a sip of his coffee. "Yeah, I don't think so."

Frank slid him a look. "What does that mean?"

"I know you, Frank, and I know you're goin' nuts over Heidi Duffin."

"I already told you guys that."

TJ came out of the cabin, and Frank handed him the third cup of coffee granules he'd prepared. "What'd I miss?"

"Nothing," Frank said at the same time Ben said, "Frank was just going to tell me about Heidi."

"I was not," Frank growled.

"Okay, okay," Ben said. "But we're here if you need us."

Frank nodded, appreciative of that above all else. He knew he wouldn't find who he was looking for in town. He should've known that from the beginning. Would've saved himself a lot of trouble.

Can't change it now, he thought as TJ started talking. This time, he said, "I've been thinking about what I could do instead of engineering."

"Oh, yeah?" Ben pulled out a package of instant oatmeal.

"Yeah. I want to brainstorm on the way back."

"Let's go out to the pond first," Frank suggested. "Then we'll go back. I want to check something out there."

"Always working," TJ teased. "This is why you're thirty and not married."

He meant it as a playful jab, Frank knew. So he chuckled with his brothers, ate his apple cinnamon oatmeal and saddled his favorite horse, Pilot. But TJ's words stung, and bit deep, and held on with sharp teeth.

Because maybe they were true.

Would he lose Heidi because he worked too much? He hadn't been over to see her in the evenings once this week. What did she think of that? He urged Pilot to walk a bit faster, suddenly eager to get to the pond, check the alkaline levels, and get back to the homestead.

And Heidi.

That evening, Frank knocked softly on Heidi's front door. He'd drawn last for a shower, so he had some time to kill. Without anywhere soft to rest in the homestead, and Heidi's goodies sitting like lead in his stomach, he'd come to visit her.

She didn't answer, and he wondered if she'd gone to bed. Surely not, as it was barely eight o'clock. He knocked again, but not much louder. A few moments later, she pulled the door all the way open.

"Hello," she said, warmth and happiness infusing her tone. Maybe he'd worried needlessly.

He drank her in like a parched man in the desert. She wore a pair of pink-and-white checkered pants with a large, matching pink sweatshirt. He swallowed when he realized he'd been staring for several long seconds.

"Evenin'." He hooked his thumb over his shoulder. "I saw the goodies you brought over."

"Yeah, I had a rough afternoon."

His eyebrows shot up, and a strong need to protect her burned a path through his bloodstream. "You bake when things get rough?" he asked, when he really wanted to know what had been rough about her day.

"Usually, yes." She shuffled her feet and kept an extra-tight grip on the door. "It calms me."

"Yeah, well, I'm all hyped up on lemon tarts and cookies. You wanna take a walk with me?"

A smile sprang to her lips, drawing Frank's attention there. She opened her mouth to say something, but emotions clouded her face. They appeared and disappeared so quickly, Frank couldn't make sense of them. She startled and fell back a step.

"You okay?" Frank reached for her, but drew his hand back before he touched her. Something wasn't right with her, and he needed to fix it.

"A walk sounds nice," she managed to say. "But I'm tired."

A frown marred his face, and he detected the notes of dishonesty in her voice. "Heidi, tell me what I did wrong."

"You didn't do anything wrong."

He reached for her again, this time moving closer and closer until he wound his fingers through hers. "I must have."

She sighed and sagged into his chest. He brought his arms around her, sure she'd be able to hear and feel the thumping of his heart. It practically leapt out of his chest at the chance to hold her tight, smell her hair, touch her so intimately.

"What's wrong?" he asked.

"It's just...you know, it's just stupid."

"Does it upset you?"

"Yes," she whispered.

"Then it's not stupid." He tilted his head and touched his lips to her temple, a thrill running down his back when she shivered in his arms. "Tell me what happened."

Another sigh, and she stepped out of his arms. The world felt cold, and empty, and utterly meaningless without her, and Frank knew everything in his life was about to change. He wanted it to change. Because he wanted Heidi in his life permanently.

She moved to the front step, keeping her hand in his, and sat down. "So I went to church today."

So far, so good. Frank had wondered if she'd go, if she went to church much. For her to go by herself spoke volumes.

"I ran into a couple of women."

Frank groaned and unconsciously squeezed her fingers.

"Apparently, you dated them all. Recently." She looked at him, the weight of her gaze on the side of his face more powerful than anything Frank had experienced before. Even when he'd shot his BB gun through the windshield of his mother's car, he hadn't received a look this huge, this heavy, this harrowed.

"I can explain about that."

"I'd love to hear it," she said.

Frank swallowed, and breathed. Breathed, and swallowed. The words he needed wouldn't come. He closed his eyes and said a prayer for help, then opened his mouth and spoke. "At the end of last year, I felt like I really needed to make more of an effort to find someone to marry."

The story poured out of him, and his appreciation for Heidi doubled when she didn't interrupt him, didn't question him, and didn't speak right away after he finished.

He wanted to tell her he felt differently about her, and that he had no idea what he was doing, and beg her for time to figure things out. But he kept silent, because if there was one thing Heidi didn't have to give him, it was time.

That's not true. The words came into his mind, but he wasn't sure how they got there. Just because she was leaving in September didn't mean they couldn't make a relationship work. He could call; she could write letters. She only had a year left, then she could come back to Three Rivers to open her bakery, come back to him.

With such clarity of thought he squeezed her hand. "Tell me what you're thinking."

She shook her head. "Too much to articulate."

"You believe me?"

"Yeah." She nodded and cuddled into his side. "Yeah, I believe you."

Relief made his sigh extra loud. "Thank the stars. I—well, what you think about me is important to me."

She let a few beats of silence go by. "So I have some questions."

His muscles tensed, but he said, "Shoot."

"I'll start with the easier ones first."

"Deal."

"Did you like the lemon tarts?"

He chuckled and enjoyed the sound of her laughter mingling with his. "Yes, they were delicious. The perfect blend of sweet and sour." He was beginning to realize how important Heidi's baking was to her. She did it when she got stressed, and his opinion on how things tasted seemed to carry a lot of weight.

"Thank you. How was your trip with your brothers?"

"Good."

"Doesn't sound like it."

"It's just complicated. We're all working through some things, and there's a lot up in the air. We'll get through. We have each other, and that helps."

She nodded an acceptance of his answer. "How's your dad doing?"

"He likes you."

"I brought him chocolate cake. Anyone would be happy to see me if I was carrying chocolate cake."

"I'm happy to see you even when you don't have chocolate cake."

Her prolonged silence made him add, "My dad is stubborn. He wants to let go of the ranch, and his life here, but he doesn't quite know how. Moving him out in January will be hard for all of us. But we all know it's the right thing to do, so we'll do it."

"And how are you doing with taking over the ranch?"

"Oh, that's the easiest one, sweetheart." His tongue tripped on the endearment. She stiffened next to him, and he tensed. In the next moment, before he could apologize, she relaxed. He said, "I've always wanted the ranch. Sure, it's a lot of work, but I love it. I have a lot to learn, and I'm sure I'll make mistakes. But I've always wanted to be a rancher. It's in my blood."

She nodded, her fingers tightening and then releasing his. Tightening and releasing. "One more question, and I think I might already know the answer."

"Might as well ask."

"Are you still looking for someone to marry?" Her voice came out strained and high-pitched.

He didn't hesitate, didn't even want to. "Yes."

She swallowed audibly. "Okay, well, that concludes the question and answer period for this evening." She started to stand, but he held her firmly in place.

"I have a couple follow-up questions."

"What if I don't want to answer them?"

"I answered yours."

"Frank, I'm—I need to go bake something."

He let her go, because her running off to bake something answered his question. It *did* scare her that he was looking long-term. But he didn't know how to think in months and not forever. At least not right now.

So he'd go slower. Not scare her off completely.

Is that what I should do? *he prayed.*

Frank had never been one to get a big, booming answer to his prayers. Sometimes he didn't even know they'd been answered until someone pointed it out to him. Sometimes he felt peaceful, and sometimes he simply knew what to do, like something had pierced his brain and eliminated all other possibilities.

Right now, he felt unsettled and distressed. Something rattled and banged in the cabin behind him, and he repeated his question for the Lord.

A thought came to his mind. *Show her a different path.*

He repeated it out loud to himself, and added, "What path?"

But God was decidedly silent on that part.

Chapter Six

Much to Heidi's simultaneous delight and horror, Frank started showing up along with the other cowhands at her house for dinner. When she looked at him with question marks in her eyes, he'd shrugged and said, "My house is torn up. Can Ben and TJ come over too?"

Of course she'd said yes. Heidi enjoyed feeding people, enjoyed it when they left happy and full, enjoyed gathering them all to her, talking with them, and then sending them back to their homes.

Friday night arrived, and Heidi decided to go into town with Chase and Matty. She didn't necessarily want to dance, but she wanted to see Maggie, talk through a few things. She finished her work as fast as possible and ran home to whip up a chocolate pie and take a shower. Both were for the benefit of Frank.

She stopped by his office close to five o'clock, because the man operated like a machine. Into work at the same time every morning. Home to tear something apart at the same time every night. She actually admired his routine, his steadiness.

"Hey." She slid the pie onto his desk and sat in the chair across from him. He glanced up at her and then down at the pie, a smile pulling at his strong mouth and crinkling his eyes. "Boy, are you a sight for sore eyes." His gaze swept her, devouring her, before returning to her face.

He took off his hat and ran his fingers through his dark hair. Heidi stared; she'd never seen him without his hat, and he completely transformed before her. The need to run her fingers through his hair suddenly seemed as important as oxygen or food. She sat on her hands instead.

"So why'd you come by bearing pie?" He settled his hat back into place, becoming the cowboy she'd started to fall for. And was deathly afraid she was falling for. She'd practically ran away from him last weekend, and she desperately needed to talk to Maggie before she did or said anything else to either bring Frank closer or push him farther away.

"I'm going into town tonight to the dance. Chase and Matty are driving me. I want to see my sister. So there's no dinner at my cabin tonight." The words rushed out of her, and she wasn't sure why she was so nervous right now.

He sat back in his chair and looked at her. He had that same penetrating gaze his father possessed, and Heidi didn't mind it with the older man. But Frank's assessment of her meant more, and she squirmed. "Well, that's all."

"Do you want to go to the dance with me?" he asked.

She did. Oh, she did. Standing in the circle of his arms had been the sweetest thing she'd experienced since getting accepted to culinary school. But she didn't know how to do that and leave in September. It didn't seem fair.

She'd prayed endlessly for the opportunity to go to school. She'd worked for it tirelessly. Did God not want her to finish?

The insertion of Frank Ackerman into her life had clouded everything. Why had God put him in her life now, if she wasn't supposed to be here with him?

"Heidi?"

She nodded. "I'd like that." She couldn't lie, and while she hadn't exactly been untruthful with herself this past week, she'd avoided doing anything about Frank. She thought about him constantly, ran through a dozen different scenarios, but she hadn't spoken to him, hadn't called Maggie, hadn't taken any action at all. Almost like he was a problem that would sort itself out if she simply gave it enough time.

But he wasn't, and sitting across from him, she realized she'd have to make a decision one way or the other pretty soon. Because the man had desire etched in every beautiful line of his face. He liked her, and he liked her a lot.

"The Fourth of July is comin' up," he said. "Maybe you'd like to go to the rodeo with me too. There's a festival, and a picnic. We could make a whole day of it."

She wanted to say yes. She did. Panic made it impossible for her vocal chords to say that one word. She pushed out of the chair, flinching when it scraped loudly on the thin carpet. "I need to talk to my sister." She turned and fled his office, not quite sure why being with him felt so right and so perfect, and yet scared her senseless.

As her footsteps beat a path back to her cabin, they seemed to be saying, *Bakery or Frank? Bakery or Frank? Bakery or Frank?*

She stumbled into her cabin and hurried into her bedroom. "Why did you bring me here?" she asked, tilting her head toward the ceiling. "Am I supposed to stay here with him?" Because she could easily see herself marrying Frank and living on this beautiful ranch for years to come.

But the constant ache for a bakery had never gone away. "Do I have to choose?" she whispered. "How do I choose?"

Something her father told her came into her mind. *Be strong.* So she wiped the few tears that had escaped and straightened. She didn't have to choose right now. She and Frank weren't really anything yet. Sure, she liked him. Liked talking to him. Liked holding his hand. Wanted to kiss him. But the fact was, she hadn't committed to him. He hadn't committed to her. Just because she held his hand didn't make them a couple.

"But you could become a couple," she said to herself. "Easily. Because you like him as much as he likes you."

She definitely needed to bake a batch of cookies before she talked with Maggie.

"How did you find time to make cookies?" Chase chuckled as Heidi adjusted the paper plate on her lap as she slid into his truck.

"There's always time for cookies." She lifted the plastic wrap and held the plate toward him.

He took one but didn't bite into it. "We waitin' for anyone else?"

"Isn't Matty coming?" She peered through the windshield but

didn't see him.

"Yeah, he'll be out in a minute." Chase slid her a glance. "What about Frank?"

Heidi flinched at the mention of his name. "Not sure." Running off before finishing the conversation could hardly be considered polite, and Heidi glanced toward the homestead. She saw no signs of life.

"You want to go check?"

She did, and she didn't. Matty came running toward the truck, opened the door and slid in beside Heidi, sandwiching her between himself and Chase. She couldn't get out now. "Let's just go," she muttered.

"All right," Chase said with a high level of unsaid implications. He put the truck in reverse and backed out of the parking lot. "You made me late, Matty."

"Oh, your girlfriend can wait." He spied the cookies on Heidi's lap. "Are those still warm?"

She handed him the plate, her mind churning and her stomach roiling. She really shouldn't have left without Frank. Or at least checking with him. Regret laced through her during the entire forty-minute drive to town. By the time Chase parked and she could get out of the cab, she felt near suffocation.

The trees towered above her, and she took a deep, calming breath. The heat of the summer hadn't dulled much, especially since the sun hadn't fully set yet. Matty sauntered off as Chase started searching the sidewalks for Maggie.

"I get to talk to her first," Heidi reminded him.

"Right after I kiss her hello," Chase countered back, a giddy grin on his face. Heidi believed that was what love looked like. She'd never felt like that about anyone, had wondered if she even could. But, now, with Frank, she got the same goofy smile whenever she saw him.

"There she is," he said, increasing his pace. "Mags!" He waved his hand, and she saw him, her face lighting up. He caught her in his arms and swung her around as she laughed. After setting her on her feet, he bent down at the same time he swiped his cowboy hat off. He kissed her, and she melted into him, and extreme jealousy roared through Heidi.

She wanted to kiss Frank like that. Right now.

Instead, she'd left him at the ranch without even checking with him first. She spun away, her heart beating irregularly. She needed to get back to the ranch. Right now.

"Chase—" she started, but got cut off by a squeal and a hug from her sister.

"It's so good to see you." Maggie held her tight, and Heidi almost started crying. She'd made friends at the ranch in the two weeks she'd been there. She wasn't that lonely. But having Maggie here meant the world, because she was family. And family had always held a special place in Heidi's heart.

"What's the matter?" Maggie asked.

"I don't know." Heidi released her sister and wiped the single tear that had crowded her right eye.

"Is it Frank?"

Heidi shook her head, then nodded, then shrugged.

"Okay, so it's Frank." She cast a glance over her shoulder to Chase. "Give us a few minutes, okay? I'll be right back."

Chase held up both his hands. "Take your time. I'll go make sure Matty is behavin' himself." He eased into the crowd in the happy-go-lucky way he had, and Heidi envied him again.

Maggie linked her arm through Heidi's and started walking down the sidewalk. "Tell me what's going on."

"I like Frank Ackerman. A lot."

Maggie stepped and stepped again. "And that's bad? Does he not like you?"

"No, he does."

"Heidi, I don't understand."

They crossed the street to a quieter patch of grass and sat down. "I don't either," Heidi started. She plucked a handful of grass and rolled it between her fingers. "He's looking for a wife. I'm scared."

Maggie stared at her for a few moments before a laugh burst from her mouth. "Oh, Heidi, you've known the man for two weeks. You're not going to marry him any time soon."

Heidi kept her eyes on the ground. "I'm not like you, Mags. I—I haven't dated anyone the way you have." With the words started, she continued on to say, "I've always wanted a bakery. I only have a year of school left. Am I supposed to give up on those things?" The all-too-familiar desperation clogged her throat, and she couldn't swallow it away no matter how hard she tried.

"So finish school. If Frank is the one, he'll wait."

She made it sound so easy. Heidi looked at her. "Is it really that easy?" Hope colored her voice.

"Why wouldn't it be?"

"It just isn't. Things aren't that simple."

Maggie smiled. A sisterly, lovely smile. "Heidi, trust me when I say it is exactly that simple. You tend to make everything more than it needs to be."

"He likes me."

"And you like him. So explore that!" Maggie threw her hands wide. "Enjoy it. This could be the best summer of your life."

Maggie had always been the more spontaneous one, the more adventurous one, the one who could drive for an hour to a dance to meet a boy she'd known for five minutes in Daddy's store.

"Promise me you won't think too hard about this," Maggie said as she stood up. She held out her hands and helped Heidi to her feet. "If you like him, and he likes you, then enjoy it. Hold his hand." She nudged Heidi with her shoulder. "Kiss him." She giggled. "See if you like him enough to make something permanent."

"But—"

"No buts." Maggie faced her and put both hands on her shoulders. "You don't have to quit school, even if you decide you want things to be long-term with Frank. This isn't a one-or-the-other scenario. You can have both."

Both. The word bounced around in Heidi's mind as she studied the horizon past Maggie.

"Uh, Heidi?"

She brought her attention back to her sister, but Maggie gazed over Heidi's shoulder, a stunned look on her face.

"What?" She twisted to see what Maggie was looking at.

But it wasn't a *what.*

It was a *who.*

It was Frank.

And he didn't look happy to see her.

Frank paused a healthy distance from Heidi and Maggie, satisfied that it was indeed them, and that Heidi had seen him.

When he'd discovered she'd left the ranch without him.... Frank had never known such a range of emotions. From disbelief, to desperation, to downright anger. He'd seriously considered never speaking to her again. He'd wondered if perhaps Heidi was just a little bit too young for him. That maybe he needed to find a woman closer to his own age, who wouldn't do something as immature as run away when conversations got difficult. Or leave him behind after he'd asked her to go to the dance with him.

She turned back to her sister, and they bent their heads together. Frank settled his weight on one foot and stuck his hands in his pockets. He'd followed her here. He wasn't going to make her talk to him if she didn't want to.

Maggie skipped away and crossed the street, and Heidi moved toward him with the speed of a sloth.

"Hey, Frank."

"Heidi."

She wiped her palms on her shorts like they were sweaty and swallowed, hard. "I'm really sorry I didn't wait for you."

"Yeah, me too." He cleared his throat. "Why didn't you wait for me?"

She inhaled and she seemed like she might start crying. Frank prayed she wouldn't. He wouldn't even know what to do with her then. A stab of empathy moved through him—he wanted to protect her from the hard things of life. Give her every day without a reason to cry. But he deserved someone who wanted to do the same for him. And he needed her to answer.

Her fingers shook as she said, "I'm scared, that's all."

"Of what?"

She lifted one shoulder in a sexy shrug. "You know." She waved her hand in the air, indicating all of Three Rivers. "Moving out here. You know, I'm not a country girl?" A nervous laugh escaped her mouth. "And you, and school, and…." Her eyes came back to his and she clamped her arms around herself. "And you."

He took a single step closer. "You're afraid of me?"

"Not you, no."

He gave his head a little shake. "Heidi, you're not makin' any sense." But he didn't need her to. He knew exactly what she was afraid of. He swept closer and drew her into a hug. "Listen, sweetheart. I just like being with you. I like talkin' to you, and I like hearing you talk back to me. This can go slow."

She leaned her cheek against his chest and held him tight. Powerful emotions dove through him, and he thought one of them might be love. But he wouldn't be telling her that.

"You said you were looking for a wife."

"I am." He rubbed a smooth circle on her back. "But that

doesn't mean I'm gonna get married tomorrow."

"I got scared."

"I know you did."

"I'm sorry."

"We'll go slower."

She tilted her head back and gazed up at him. "I—well, I'm not really good at dating. Haven't really found anyone I'm interested in spending more than five minutes with—until you."

"I'm glad you tacked that last bit on the end." He grinned down at her.

"I'm just not very good at this. Will you forgive me for running off?"

"Will you bring me a chocolate cake tomorrow?"

A smile finally lit up her face, and Frank abandoned his idea to take things slow. He didn't care that he stood in the middle of town, in broad daylight.

He bent down and lightly touched his lips to Heidi's, sure she'd freak out and scamper away to her sister.

But she didn't. Her hands rose over his chest and settled around his neck, and he pulled off his cowboy hat with one hand while keeping her securely against him with the other, and kissed her like he meant it this time.

An hour later, he held her on the dance floor, twirling her, and laughing with her, and enjoying his time with her. He hadn't kissed a woman in a while, and he knew he'd never kiss another one.

Because kissing Heidi had changed him. Healed some broken parts of him, and caused others to crack. He'd felt himself falling as he kissed her, and now that he had, it was all he could think about.

"C'mon," he said after the song ended. "I'm hot."

She exhaled heavily next to him. "Let's get a drink."

"Let's get out of here." He glanced at her. "We can grab ice cream on the way back to the ranch. You want to?"

"Do we have to go to that same place?"

He'd managed to keep the women away from Heidi tonight, but they'd both seen them circling. It wasn't hard to miss Whitney's glare or Claire's poutiness. Frank had even considered paying Matty to dance with one of them but they'd left before he could.

"Nah, we'll go through the drive-through and grab something."

Heidi wrinkled her nose.

"Oh, I suppose you could whip us up something better in about ten seconds." He slid his arm around her shoulders when they broke free of the crowd.

She leaned into him. "Maybe not ten seconds."

"Well, I need something to drink before I drive home. Where do you want to go?"

"Anywhere Victoria isn't."

Frank chuckled and pulled Heidi behind a tree. He cupped her face in his hands and smiled. "Tonight didn't turn out too bad, right?"

She pressed her back into the bark and slipped her hands to his shoulders. "Not too bad at all." She gripped his cowboy hat and lifted it off his head, dropping the hand holding it to her side. With her other hand, she slid her fingers through his hair.

Every nerve ending stood at attention, and Frank had a hard time breathing properly. The touch felt so intimate, so sincere, and he wanted more of it. "Heidi," he whispered.

"Yeah?"

But he didn't really have anything to say. So he kissed her again, hoping that actions could speak louder than words. Hers certainly did, because he felt things in her reciprocated touch he didn't think she'd ever say. At least not right now.

"Is this how you go slower?" she asked as he trailed his lips along her jawline toward her neck.

He pulled back and found her eyes in the dim light. They sparkled with a tease and something deeper. "Sorry," he said. "I'll behave myself." He put space between them and reached for her hand. "So tell me. How long is your last year of school? Are we talkin' like a full calendar year? Or a couple of semesters?"

Because he knew he wouldn't ask her to stay when it was time for her to leave. He'd already promised her that, and he was a man of his word. But he needed to know how long he'd have to wait for her to come back. He needed time to prepare himself mentally.

"A couple of semesters."

"Mm." He unlocked his truck and opened her door for her. He could have the house done by the time she returned. Maybe then she'd be ready to think long-term with him, though if her kisses were anything to go by, she already was.

He put the passion in her kisses from his mind long enough to swing by a fast-food restaurant and grab a couple of ice cream cones and drive home. By the time he pulled into his driveway, though, the desire to hold her close and breathe her in almost suffocated him.

Ben and his near-fiancé, Rebecca, sat on the front porch, their knees touching and their heads bent together. Frank watched them for a moment, lost inside a fantasyland where he and Heidi shared every detail of their lives together.

"You getting out?" she asked.

He glanced over and realized she'd already slid from the truck. He unbuckled his seatbelt and got out. She met him at the front of the truck and slipped her hand into his before turning to face the house.

Ben glanced up as Frank and Heidi approached, a grin already on his face. He took in their joined hands, and his eyes widened a hair. Enough for Frank to see, though.

"Hey, guys." Ben gestured to Heidi. "Becca, this is...." He swallowed hard, but Frank's own pulse had just tripled. How would he introduce Heidi from now on?

"I'm Heidi Duffin." She released Frank's hand and stepped forward. "Frank hired me to clean the cowboy cabins."

"Nice to meet you." Becca smiled in that easy way she had, but Frank couldn't look away from his brother. He couldn't seem to get his voice or his feet to work.

"Maybe you'd like to walk me back to my cabin, Frank."

In slow motion, like someone had half-frozen time, he turned his head to look at her. She gazed up at him expectantly.

"Walk the girl home, Frank," Ben said, launching Frank into

motion.

"Good to see you again, Becca." Frank moved away, glad his body seemed to be responding again.

Heidi claimed his hand again and said, "She seems nice."

"She is."

"They're serious?" She glanced over her shoulder, where Ben and Becca had resumed their private conversation.

"They'll probably get engaged before summer ends." Frank felt the weight of his words. It had never bothered him that his younger brothers might marry before him. But somehow, now it nagged at him. "Ben only has one year of dental school left, and Becca will want to get married here before they move to Dallas."

"Have they been together long?"

"Maybe a year?" Frank guessed. "I don't know." His feet crunched on the gravel path, but he didn't want to lose Heidi to her cabin. "It's nice tonight," he said. "You want to keep walking? We can go out to the bull pens."

"How far is it?"

"Maybe a half a mile. There's a road."

"I can do a half a mile."

He smiled and leaned toward her, stealing a breath of her strawberry-scented hair. "All right, then." He took her around the back of the cabins instead of down the path between them and the other ranch buildings. The range spread before them, alight with the glow of the moon.

"It's beautiful here," Heidi sighed, pausing her stride to stare out into the wilderness.

"I'm glad you think so." He listened to the night sounds of the country. "That's probably the best compliment a city girl could give a ranch."

"Hey."

"I was joking. C'mon." He tugged on her hand to get her moving again. "I don't mind that you're a city girl."

"Horses are big animals, you know. They terrify me the littlest bit."

"Well, they're terrified of you the littlest bit too."

"We don't even have a dog."

"I have two." Frank turned toward the cabins, but they'd only passed a couple. "Want to meet them?"

"Two at the same time?"

"They're calm. And small. A lot smaller than horses, though you could meet mine if you wanted."

"What's his name?"

"Pilot. C'mon, he'll love you."

"Can horses actually do that?"

"Of course. Horses are very loyal animals." He led her through the alleyway between two cabins and toward the horse barn. Locked up for the night, he turned while he thought. "Let me grab my keys." He dropped her hand and spun in the direction of the homestead.

"You're going to leave me out here alone?" The panic in Heidi's voice wasn't hard to hear.

"No," Frank said smoothly. "Come on back to the house with me. You can see the progress I've made. Then we'll come back over to get the dogs out."

She tucked herself into his side, and Frank liked the feel of her there. His mind raced and his pulse clashed as he tried to figure out how to keep her in his life past the summer.

Show her a different path. Those words had plagued him for almost a week, and he still didn't know what they meant. He just needed more time to figure it out. Too bad time was the one thing going against him.

Heidi stopped just inside the backdoor, where Frank had tacked a huge blueprint to the wall. The bare bulb above it illuminated the drawing, and she sucked in a breath when she found the enormous kitchen, the long island down the middle of it, an expansive eat-in dining area.

"Frank, is this what you're doing to the house?"

He searched for the keys on a rack next to the drawing. He plucked a set from the peg and joined her. "Yeah, we're starting the excavation on Monday. Then we'll frame, and go from there."

She reached up and traced her fingertips down the line separating the garage from the house, her breath caught somewhere in her throat. "The whole thing will be different."

"Better," Frank said.

"Why is rebuilding the homestead so important to you?" She pulled her attention from the blueprint to focus on Frank.

He shifted his feet, almost imperceptibly, almost like he didn't want her to see it. But Heidi saw everything about Frank, right down to the sexy stubble on his jawline and the ring of anxiety in his blazing eyes.

"I told you," he said.

"Tell me again."

"My mother—"

"Died a decade ago."

He sucked in a breath, and Heidi wondered if she'd crossed a line. She put her hand on his forearm, which felt tight, tight, tight because of the way he held his fingers in a fist.

"Why is it important to *you*?"

He drew a deep breath, steadfastly refusing to look at her. "Because Three Rivers Ranch used to be a community of sorts. A family. And I want to establish that again. My father, he's…he doesn't know how to do it. I don't really either, but I see what you've done in the two short weeks you've been here, and I need a bigger, nicer place to do it."

Confusion muddled Heidi's thoughts. "What have I done?"

He swung his eyes toward hers, grabbing them and holding on. "You haven't noticed the twenty-five men you feed each evening?"

Heat rose through her body, touching her face and making it flame. "That's, well, that's nothing. Me cooking too much."

He shook his head. "No, Miss Heidi, that's called building a community. Momma always said it started with food, and well, you've seen how well we eat around here."

She glanced back at the drawing of the giant kitchen on the wall. "Just having a bigger kitchen won't make the food cook itself."

"I know." He reached for the doorknob and exited the house.

"So who's gonna feed everyone once I'm gone?" She wasn't sure why she was pressing the issue. Did she want him to beg her to stay? Ask her to marry him right now? Both of those things struck fear in her heart and caused her chest to tighten. She didn't know what she wanted anymore, and she hated the mixed up feelings swirling through her.

He cut her a glance from the corner of his eye, too short for her to read anything into it. "I'll find someone," he said.

Her heart fell, fell, fell. Crashed to the ground. Burned, and blistered, and bubbled with hurt.

He'd find someone?

She stopped walking, but it took him a couple of strides to notice. "Heidi?"

"I am the flavor of the month, aren't I?"

A hard edge entered his expression. "Absolutely not." He closed the distance between them and gathered her into his arms. Safety descended upon her, and her doubts about Frank dried up.

"Heidi, when I think of who I want in that kitchen, helpin' me make this ranch a family, it's you." His soft, deep voice vibrated through her ears, her chest, her very soul. "But I promised you I wouldn't ask you to stay when it was time to go, and well, to be honest, I've known you for three weeks, and this could end differently than I can see right now."

She didn't want it to end at all, but she kept the words buried deep.

"I'm not interested in anyone else, okay?"

She nodded against his chest, but he backed up and lifted her chin with two strong fingers. "Okay?"

"Okay, Frank."

He gave her that dazzling smile—the one that could brighten the darkest day—and his eyes drifted closed as he leaned down and pressed his lips to hers.

She drank him in greedily, her fingers finding the soft hair at the back of his neck. Kissing Frank Ackerman had ruined her for life, she was sure. No other man would ever be able to make her feel as alive as he did. As adored. As cherished.

The man had a way of saying all kinds of things without uttering a word. She kissed him, and kissed him, and kissed him and still couldn't get enough.

Heidi slept in on Saturday, her night with Frank the previous evening going until almost midnight. She hadn't freaked out too badly over the dogs, and they did genuinely seem to like her. Of the two, she preferred Duke, the tri-colored Australian shepherd. He'd licked her hand and sat back on his haunches like they were old pals that had been separated for a while. Daisy had been more excited to meet Heidi, and she sniffed and licked and jumped up on Heidi, who didn't quite know what to do with the animal.

But Frank looked at the dogs with complete affection, scratching under their jaws and giving them treats. He'd kissed her good-night on her front porch, and again, Heidi wondered what it felt like to fall in love.

She'd never done it before, and she wasn't sure if this floaty, numb feeling would wear off or last forever. She got up and began tidying up her own cabin, as she didn't have much time during the week to attend to her own house.

Her thoughts took her to San Francisco, of her friends there, her remaining classes. Could she return to school and keep a relationship with Frank? She barely knew the rules of dating in person, let alone across hundreds of miles.

She switched off her worries when she switched off the vacuum cleaner. She'd felt at peace when Maggie had said she could have both Frank and finish school. Did she believe it or not?

She did.

She just needed to have more faith. She squared her shoulders, poured herself a bowl of cereal, and wandered onto her porch when loud noises began to echo through the quiet countryside.

Frank had been busy this morning already. She wasn't sure why she expected anything different. He poked his head out the driver's side window of his truck while Ben directed him to back a huge trailer filled with lumber onto the lawn.

She settled into the rocking chair and watched the two men unload the lumber. Well, she admired Frank's strong muscles as he pulled and lifted and moved armful after armful. Though it was only mid-morning, Heidi felt as though she sat on the surface of the sun. Sure, Texas in June was hot, but Frank Ackerman....

Heidi shivered. As if summoned by her flirty thoughts, Frank glanced toward her cabin. When he saw her sitting there, he lifted one of his gloved hands in hello, a broad smile stretching across his face.

She got up and leaned against the railing closest to the homestead. "Morning, Frank. Hey, Ben."

Frank said something to his brother, who smiled and waved in Heidi's direction, and then came toward her with long strides. Her heart thu-thumped in time with his cowboy boots, increasing when he moved right up to the railing, pulling his cowboy hat off and tipping his head back to receive her kiss.

She giggled against his lips, glad when he added his chuckle to the mix. "You're sweaty," she said.

"Some of us have been workin'."

"It's the weekend," she said as he moved around to the front steps and came up to claim her in his arms.

"Ranch work doesn't care what day of the week it is."

"I've noticed that." And she didn't like it, though she knew owning a bakery would be the same way. And there'd be no sleeping in then, ever.

The reality of a bakery had never seemed so far away, though she'd never been closer. But as she enjoyed the comfort and security of Frank's embrace, her bakery faded to a distant dot on a distant horizon.

Days blended into weeks, with cleaning and watching Frank's land and house transform, and kissing him every chance she got. She'd kissed him in his office with her back pressed against the closed door as he held her close with his strong hands. And in the horse barn when they went to visit the dogs. On her front porch. In his mudroom, with the blueprint over her shoulder.

Her favorite place was out on the range, under the wide sky and in time with the lilting breeze.

"Picnic this weekend," Frank said one day when she stopped by his office just as he was getting ready to leave. "Rodeo Friday night?" He stuck some papers in a folder and glanced up.

"I've never been to a rodeo," she admitted.

He stared at her like she'd just told him she'd come from another planet. "What, now?"

She smirked at him. "You heard me."

"But you grew up in Amarillo."

"So?"

"So, they put on a great rodeo every year."

"Remember how I don't like horses, or cows, or—"

He held up his hand. "I remember how you didn't *used to* like those things." He flashed her a smile. "Rodeo on Friday. It'll change your life."

"I highly doubt that."

"Well, at the very least, I'll buy you some nachos."

She wrinkled her nose. "That's not real food."

"Stop it." He stalked closer to her. "Tell me you've had nachos before."

"Of course I have."

"From a fair or a circus or something."

"That's not real food," she insisted.

A devilish grin stole across his breathtaking face. "Oh, we're gonna have a great weekend. So much culture."

Heidi groaned, simply to make Frank growl. When he did, a thrill of delight squirreled down her spine. He tickled her, and she leapt away from him, pulling on the doorknob to escape his office. "Dinner at six," she called over her shoulder, still laughing. When she got to the exit, she turned back to see him leaning in his office doorway, those intense blue eyes dancing with amusement as he watched her.

She ducked outside, flushed and overly hot though the administration building had air conditioning. Frank was really good at making her internal temperature rise, and with every passing day she spent with him, she fell a little deeper toward loving him.

She loved the ranch, everything about it. She'd walked with him out to the bullpens one night, then gone with him on a three-wheeler out to a cabin about a half-hour's ride away. They'd spent an afternoon there, talking about what Pastor Allan had said in church earlier that day.

Heidi had enjoyed her summer so far, just as Maggie had suggested she do. No promises were made. They didn't talk much about her school after he'd asked how much longer she had until she graduated. But it was an ever-present being in their relationship. An invisible giant just waiting to snatch her away.

"But not for good," she told herself as she stirred the pot of baked beans. It was the first time she'd thought she could leave Three Rivers Ranch, leave Frank, and come back.

But that meant…"No bakery." Her voice sounded haunted in the empty kitchen where she worked, preparing a meal for the cowhands who had come to expect dinner on a nightly basis.

Frank had been buying the groceries for weeks now, thank goodness. Heidi just made the food. But everyone flocked to her cabin at six o'clock, even if their chores weren't done. They'd eat and talk and laugh and then head back to out to fix the tractor they'd been working on, or finish feeding the calves, or baling the hay in the surrounding pastures.

Those that didn't have to go back to work would stay longer, lounging on the steps or the nearby lawn of the homestead. Frank had re-landscaped the yard so it sloped gently downward now, toward a dug out basement. He'd put in a new door and patio pavers, and the skeleton of the deck and the new, expanded upper level of the house had gone up last week.

Heidi watched it all with interest. As much as she didn't want to admit it, she could picture herself living in that house, with Frank. Gathering all the men to the deck and large kitchen for lunch, or dinner, or special barbeques for their birthdays. The thought brought her peace, and happiness, and she wondered if this dream of building a familial community at the ranch could replace the one where she owned her bakery.

Noise outside her cabin jolted her from her thoughts, and she threw several pounds of ground beef—home grown—into a cast iron skillet. Chase and a couple other men always set up the tables and chairs just before dinner, and she'd lost herself to her circular thoughts again and was now running late.

Someone knocked on her cabin door, and she called, "Come in!" so she wouldn't have to stop working. She diced an onion as she glanced up to see Frank loitering in the doorway. He never came in her house, and when she'd asked him why, he'd said, "Don't want anyone to get the wrong idea about us."

But she'd gone in his house, and everyone saw her go in his office and walk around the ranch with his hand in hers.

"Just wanted you to know my dad's comin' tonight. He's a sucker for a good baked bean, and Ben's been tellin' him about yours for two straight weeks."

A blip of anxiety bolted through her. "That'll be fun." She tossed the onions in with the meat and salted it all before adding pepper too. "This'll be done in fifteen minutes." Maybe. She cranked the flame under the pan. "You can take the baked beans out now. And the buns."

He came in, his footsteps sure and strong. Being so close to him in such a small space set her nerves on fire.

"Heidi," he said real quiet, like there might be people listening in. "Thank you."

She turned from her task at the stove, seeking his face to understand the deep river of emotion in his voice. She'd never seen Frank cry, or even get that angry. He operated on an even keel, only showing his desire and joy when they were together.

He looked at her with all seriousness in his eyes, and she said, "You're welcome."

Clearing his throat, he collected the pot of baked beans and left the kitchen. When he returned for the buns and serving utensils, he said, "Oh, and I have your paycheck from June."

Elbow-deep in sloppy Joes, she said, "Leave it on the table, would you?"

He did and went outside with everything. A few minutes later, with everything ready, she called him back in to carry the heavy pan outside too. He set it on a square of wood she'd claimed from the scrap pile and called everyone together.

"Let's pray," he said. Even those cowboys who didn't go to church swiped their hats off and bowed their heads. Heidi's heart swelled with love as Frank said grace, marveling at his strength and faith. When he finished, she realized she had tears gathering in the corners of her eyes.

She turned away from him quickly and placed the serving spoons in the sloppy Joe mix and the baked beans. The men came up the steps and went down both sides of the table, each of them saying, "Thank you, Heidi," as they passed her.

Chase gave her a quick side-hug before he went through the line and asked, "How's Maggie?"

"I haven't talked to her in a while," Heidi admitted.

"That's why I asked." He gave her a pointed look, picked up a paper plate and moved down the table.

Regret and horror snaked through her, and for the second time in ten minutes, tears crowded her eyes. She turned away from the group and slipped down the steps. She made it around to the back of her cabin, her face to the wide-open range before the first tear fell.

Several minutes passed, and while she managed to tame the tears, the raging emotions teemed inside her, pushing and pulling and prodding at her until she felt wrung out. She heard Frank calling her name, but she didn't want to be found right now, least of all by him.

Then she remembered that his father had come to dinner. She

just didn't know if she had the fortitude to face them. Frank would know instantly that she was upset, and he'd want to fix it. But he couldn't fix this situation. He couldn't fix her.

Frank's anxiety grew exponentially with every passing moment. No one had seen where Heidi went. It seemed impossible that the person who provided twenty-five men with dinner could go unnoticed for even a moment.

Anger burned through him. Had someone said something to her? She'd seemed distracted in her kitchen, something he thought couldn't happen. Had he upset her somehow? Was she nervous about his father coming to dinner?

And where in the world had she gone? He'd checked inside her cabin, even going so far as to knock on her bedroom door and open it. He'd practically ran out of the house when she wasn't there.

"Ben," he said, and Frank didn't have to say anything else.

While Ben did the same thing, Frank turned and gathered three men together for a quick discussion about where they should look before sending them off. He'd taken two steps toward the homestead, thinking maybe she'd gone there to escape the noise and chaos at her cabin when he caught movement to his right.

He turned and there she stood. "Heidi," he breathed, rushing toward her. Before he reached her, he saw she'd been crying. His heart twisted and back-flipped and everything in him wanted to make sure she never had reason to cry again.

"What's wrong?" He gathered her close, closer, stroking her hair and holding her tight as her shoulders shook. Wanting to shield her from the other men, he pulled back and said, "Stay here. I'll be right back."

He ducked around the front of the house and caught Ben by whistling as he started to go into the horse barn. His brother came back out, and Frank waved both hands above his head, a symbol the boys had used in irrigation for years. It meant, "Water's here. All's well."

Ben strode toward him. "You found her?"

"She's upset. Can you let everyone know she's okay, and they can go back to eating?"

"I'll take care of it."

"Dad still needs to come over." Frank felt pulled in a dozen different directions. "He needs help crossing the lawn. It's too uneven for him."

"Frank, I'll take care of all of it."

Gratitude filled Frank. "Thanks, Ben." He returned to Heidi, gently guiding her around the cabin and away from the crowd. She'd stopped crying, but her eyes were puffy and red.

"You wanna walk?" he asked.

She nodded and took off at a pace he'd never seen from her. He kept up easily, giving her a few minutes to slow down and settle.

"You wanna talk about it?" he asked.

"It's stupid," she said, her voice much too high. "And I'm crying over it." She shook her head, an angry blaze in her eyes that actually struck fear in Frank's core.

"I'm sure it's not stupid," he said. "Tell me about it."

"I'm just tired," she said.

"Heidi, come on."

She stopped suddenly and faced him. "I just—everything I feel is so close to the surface, you know? And Chase asked about Maggie, and I said I hadn't talked to her in a while, and he made it sound like she was upset about that, and she probably is, because I told her I'd call." She took a deep breath that shuddered through her chest.

Frank clenched his teeth, wondering why Chase felt it his duty to lecture Heidi about calling her sister. "We can go to the homestead and call her right now."

"And you know why I haven't called her?" she continued as if he hadn't even spoken. "Because I don't need her. I've been having such a great time, and everything has been going so well, and I usually need Maggie when things *aren't* going so well." She exhaled, her tears completely gone now. "So wouldn't she already know how things are here? I don't know. It shouldn't have bothered me, but—" She froze, then shook her head.

"But what?" he asked.

"I don't know."

She never let him get away with that, but Frank wasn't sure if now was the right time to push her. "What do you need from me?"

She stepped into his arms and tucked herself against his chest. "Just this." She relaxed in his embrace, and Frank knew his life would never be complete without her in it. He hadn't admitted to himself that he loved Heidi Duffin, but with her claiming him as what she needed, he realized with everything in him that he was, in fact, in love with Heidi Duffin.

His heart jumped and a pronounced sense of joy descended on him. He smiled a small little grin of gratitude to the Lord for bringing Heidi into his life. "It's okay," he whispered. "I'm right here, and everything is okay."

Frank fretted about Heidi for a few days, though she insisted she was feeling better. She'd called Maggie, she assured him, and she'd apologized—apologized!—for breaking down over something so little.

He wanted to tell her that whatever bothered her was fine, that she could break down any time she wanted. Instead, he poured his energy into making sure everything would go as well as possible for the Fourth of July celebrations in town. He'd bought tickets to the rodeo in the center section, and called Miss Frannie to make sure she was bringing her world-famous potato salad and pork ribs to the barbeque on Saturday afternoon.

She'd grilled him about himself, the ranch, his brother, their dad. Frank gave her all the answers she wanted, knowing she cared about him and their family even after all these years.

He left his desk early on Friday and headed toward the homestead. As he approached Heidi's cabin, he heard the radio playing through the open door.

Pausing at the bottom of the steps, he heard Heidi singing along with the song in a beautiful alto voice. A smile danced across his face, and he practically stomped up the steps so she'd hear him.

She kept singing, and he knocked on the door as he poked his head through the doorway. "Hello?"

Heidi sat at the sewing machine, bent over as she sang and threaded fabric under the needle. He watched her work, utterly transfixed by her beauty and resourcefulness. Her lyrics faded into a hum and the sewing machine stopped. She lifted the foot, and he said, "You have a nice voice."

She yelped and jumped and her garment went flying. Her gaze met his, and she pressed one hand to her chest. "Frank, don't sneak up on me like that."

"I knocked and everything." He flashed her a smile. "What're you makin'?"

"A new skirt." She held it up to her waist. "Do you like it?"

The red fabric reminded him of the American flag, and he could only imagine what she'd pair the skirt with. "Yeah," he choked out. "It's real nice."

"I just need to finish the hem and add a waistband."

"Sounds great."

"Then I'll change, and we can go."

He'd started to turn toward the door. "Wait. You're going to wear it tonight?"

"Of course." She positioned the fabric under the foot again. "It's red and white, and I have the cutest denim jacket to wear with it. Red, white, and blue." She tossed him a quick smile and started sewing again.

He marveled at her as he strode across the lawn to the

homestead. Who could decide mid-afternoon to make a skirt to wear that evening? If he didn't hurry, she'd probably have a batch of cookies baked by the time he returned to pick her up.

She waited on the porch when he came back, wearing that sexy red skirt with a white blouse tucked into one side so he could see the white waistband. Over that, she wore the jean jacket and had slipped on a pair of white sandals.

Her hair flowed over her shoulders in loose curls and her eyes shone like stars. He whistled as he swooped up the stairs and gathered her in his arms. "You look great." He kissed her, taking his time to truly savor the feel of her lips against his, the warmth of her body pressed into him, the powdery smell of her skin and perfume.

"You might be too hot tonight," he murmured once he'd pulled away.

"You said we'd be sittin' in the shade."

He noticed her country twang, and a slip of adoration moved through him. "We will be. But it's still hot."

"I'll be fine." She started down the steps, leaving him to follow in her wake. Which he gladly did. He just wanted to be wherever Heidi was. The drive to town passed in a blink, with easy conversation, and Heidi's leg pressing against his, and her laughter ringing in his ears.

They went into the stands hand-in-hand, and Frank kept his head held high, despite the daggered looks some of the women threw his way.

They waited in the concessions line while Frank jabbered about the events, and the cowboys he knew on the rodeo circuit, and how his father had sold a bull to the rodeo years ago. He got up to the window and ordered hamburgers for both of them, as well as nachos, a churro, and sodas.

When Heidi saw all the food, her eyes widened and she looked at him. "I need help carryin' all this." He grinned and she burst into laughter.

After she took a soda and the churro, she said, "I'm still not convinced this is real food."

He picked up the box they'd stacked the food in. "The burgers are. And that there churro is a game-changer."

"You said that about the nachos."

"No, I said the nachos were life-changing." He used the cardboard tray to point toward where she needed to go. "And they are."

He switched places with her so he could lead her to their seats. The shade had already arrived and he settled onto the bench and offered her a hamburger.

But she smiled, hunched her shoulders, and wiped the cinnamon-sugar from her lips. He chuckled, the sound growing into a full laugh when he realized she'd eaten the entire churro on the walk to their seats.

"Okay, so someone's hungry," he said, still laughing.

"This has totally changed my game." She balled up the paper wrapper and tossed it in the box.

"Do you have room to eat 'real food'?" He picked up a burger and unwrapped it.

She crossed her legs, completely distracting him. "No, I think I'll change my life now." She reached for the tray of nachos. "I dip the chips in that?" She eyed the cheese sauce like it was toxic. It probably was. Frank didn't care. He loved the stuff.

"That's right." He bit into his burger—another of his favorite foods. He pretended like he wasn't watching her dip her chip and lift it toward her mouth. She finally put the whole thing in her mouth, and he abandoned his burger to gauge her reaction. She gave nothing away as she chewed and swallowed.

"Well?"

She focused on the nachos, a tiny smirk riding on her mouth, and picked up another chip. "I don't know if I'd categorize it as *life-changing*." She dipped the chip in the nacho cheese sauce.

"Did you mean to drown that chip in cheese sauce?"

She looked at it and stuck it in her mouth before it could drip onto her clothes. "It's good." After she swallowed, she added, "But I've had more life-changings things happen to me."

"Really? Like what?" In the arena below, the tractor smoothing the dirt rumbled out the door. The rodeo was about to start.

"Things," she said in an evasive voice, her face reddening. "Maggie's here somewhere."

"What kind of things?" Frank asked again, his internal temperature rising with her blush.

But she was saved from answering by the announcer declaring the start of the rodeo. He told everyone to stand for the American flag, and Frank set his burger in the box and stood, his hand on his heart as a horseback rider came flying into the arena, the Stars and

Stripes rippling as she raced around the edge of the arena.

The crowd said the Pledge of Allegiance, and the *Star Spangled Banner* was sung by a twelve-year-old who'd won a school contest.

Frank really wanted to press Heidi about what had changed her life, but he never got the chance. He did get the opportunity to laugh with her, talk with her, hold her hand, and kiss her. Phase One of giving her the perfect weekend had succeeded, and Frank floated back to his place after a bone-melting kiss with Heidi that had definitely changed his life.

Chapter Eight

Heidi found Maggie inside her cabin, pulling her hair from its French braid. "Hey!" She engulfed her sister in a hug, a million emotions about seeing her tumbling through her.

"Hey, yourself." Maggie giggled, hugged Heidi back, and then pulled away to look at her. "Wow, you're glowing."

Heidi shrugged and headed into the kitchen to make chocolate milk. "Want some?" She pulled out the powder and the milk.

"Of course." Maggie sat at the kitchen table while Heidi brought everything over to the table. "Did you like the rodeo?"

"You know, it was pretty amazing." Heidi placed two tall glasses on the table and sat across from her sister. "I liked the fireworks the best."

"Yeah, I'll bet." Maggie poured herself some milk and pushed the container toward Heidi.

"What does that mean?"

Maggie grinned and spooned powder into her glass. She started stirring before saying, "It means I saw you kissing Frank on the front porch."

Horror struck Heidi right behind her breastbone. It quickly

faded, though, as she realized she'd been kissing Frank out in the open for a couple of weeks now. Surely every cowhand at Three Rivers knew about their relationship. They hadn't exactly tried to hide it.

Still, something about having someone watch her melt into Frank made Heidi squirm.

"There were definitely fireworks," Maggie said.

Heidi laughed, the previous joy of being in Frank's arms, feeling the adoration and love in his embrace, returning in full force. "I guess there are."

"So you love him."

Heidi shook her head in time to stirring the powder into her milk. "No, I don't think I'm quite in love with him."

"What are you going to do about school?"

Heidi straightened and took a gulp of chocolate milk for strength. It slid down her throat and cooled her off. "I'm going to go. I've always wanted to finish school, and that hasn't changed."

Maggie nodded and gave her an encouraging smile. "So you've decided. Last time we talked, you hadn't."

Last time they'd talked, Heidi had barely been able to say anything besides an apology for not calling. Maggie hadn't acted like it was a big deal, and she'd spent the conversation detailing how she felt about Chase.

Heidi had learned valuable lessons from that experience. One, Maggie needed her just as much as Heidi needed Maggie. She should call, even if things were going great for her, because maybe Maggie needed to talk.

Two, Frank was kind, and caring, and wonderful in a crisis. He soothed the wounds in her soul, and held her hand, and offered whatever support he could. She'd leaned on him for a few days, and he'd gotten her through a rough emotional patch without running for the hills.

"I've decided, yes," Heidi said, her gaze wandering toward the front door.

"What about Frank?"

That was the question of the century. She stirred and drank, her thoughts meandering down the same path they always did when she thought, *What about Frank?*

"I'm hoping Frank will wait." She spoke to her milk, her voice quiet and calm. She glanced up at Maggie. "Do you think that's the right thing to do? Ask him to wait for me to finish school?"

Maggie looked at her with bright, unassuming eyes. "I can't tell you what's right for you, Heidi."

Heidi sighed and leaned back in her chair. "Yeah, I know. It just seems—well, it almost feels unfair to have met him right now. I hope that doesn't sound ungrateful. I just don't understand why God's given me both of these opportunities at the same time." The familiar desperation she'd been fighting for weeks rose to color her voice. "I felt strongly I should finish school *before* I met Frank. I—I have to stick with that. Otherwise, what was that feeling?" She looked helplessly at Maggie, who gazed back at her sympathetically and placed her hand over Heidi's.

"You have to trust those feelings."

"How do I do that? How can I know they're right?" She took a deep breath to drive the confusion away. When she let it cloud her mind, she went into a tailspin, and she didn't want to go there again.

"You know," Maggie insisted. She pulled her hand back. "You know, Heidi. You've always had great faith. Now you have to use it."

"It's hard."

Maggie finished her chocolate milk. "Daddy always said we'd have to rely on our faith in hard times."

Heidi heard their father's voice telling them that over dinner. A rush of affection for her family flowed through her, and she drained the last of her sweet treat too. "So tell me about you and Chase. Things going okay? Getting serious?"

Maggie grinned and then giggled. "Not too serious yet, Heidi. We've only been dating for a few weeks."

"*Five* weeks."

"Okay, five weeks. But I don't get to see him everyday like you see Frank. It's a little slower."

"He seems to like you." Heidi collected the dirty glasses and took them to the sink. She'd wash them in the morning. She put the milk in the fridge and the chocolate powder in the cupboard. "You guys going to the fair and picnic tomorrow?"

"Yes." Maggie got up and joined Heidi as they went into the bedroom to change. "He's taking me home after church on Sunday. Daddy got all bug-eyed when I told him that."

"Yeah, tell me how Mom and Daddy took you spending the weekend with your cowboy boyfriend they didn't know about."

She tacked a smile onto the end of her sentence, hoping it hadn't been too bad for Maggie.

"Oh, you know Momma and Daddy." She slipped into her nightgown and pulled down one side of Heidi's bed.

"So Momma asked a hundred questions while Daddy sat and listened, a growly look on his face."

Maggie laughed and laughed. "And then Daddy said—"

"I need to meet this boy," both girls said in a low voice, imitating their father. They dissolved into giggles, and Heidi felt more at peace than she had since driving to Three Rivers with Maggie all those weeks ago.

And she knew without a doubt that things would work out with Frank. She didn't know if that meant they could be together, or that he'd wait for her. But she knew whatever happened with him would be the right thing for her.

As Maggie clicked off the lamp and the girls settled into sleep, Heidi offered a prayer of gratitude for this moment of clarity. She slept the best she had since coming to the ranch.

The next afternoon, Heidi slid out of Frank's truck after him, tugging at the bottom of her dress to get it to fall into an appropriate place. The bright yellow fabric had little red cherries covering it, and she carried the light sweater she usually wore with it. But with the summer heat, she let the sun touch her bare shoulders as she faced the park.

She'd seen it filled with people during the dances, but this had gone to a completely new level. Now, kids ran and yelled. Parents hovered around the tables, setting down the dishes they'd brought to share. Elderly people sat in the shade, talking. There seemed to be activity everywhere, and Heidi felt more overwhelmed than she had last night in the crowded rodeo.

Crowds usually didn't bother her. After all, she loved the vibrancy of the city, it's hustle and bustle. But here, she felt like an outsider, someone who didn't quite belong though the Ackerman's were Three Rivers royalty.

Thankfully, Frank took her hand in one of his, carrying the platter of macaroons she'd made in the other. She felt naked, exposed, as they moved through the crowd to the dessert tables. He dropped her hand and nudged a cake to the right and a cobbler to the left to make room for their treats. The colorful macaroons definitely brightened the table, and some of Heidi's unease ebbed away.

"That's Vince Garrison." He pointed to a man about his age. "He owns the grocer. Well, his father does, but he's set to take it over."

Heidi nodded, trying to absorb all the names and faces as Frank pointed them out. She met school teachers, and the librarian, an elderly gentleman who begged Frank to come take over the barber shop. Frank laughed at that. "Just because I cut my own hair doesn't make me a barber," he told the man. "But nice try, Elliot."

"You cut your own hair?" Heidi asked as they moved away. She didn't get to see it that often—the man seemed glued to his cowboy hat.

"Well, I'm not gonna drive forty minutes for a ten-minute haircut." He slid her a grin that set her stomach on fire. "Do you cut hair, Heidi?"

"Sure," she said. "I mean, I've done it a few times for my father. This guy in San Francisco." She clamped her lips shut. She hadn't talked about her life in San Francisco much. Okay, at all. Frank didn't ask, and it sort of loomed around them like a third presence. Not so much recently, but now it rushed back, inserting awkwardness between them.

"A guy in San Francisco?" Frank's voice strayed into a higher octave, and he wouldn't look at her.

She found him adorable, the way he was interested but wanted to pretend like he wasn't. "Yeah, I have friends in San Francisco," she said. "Some of them are male." Most weren't, but Frank would have to ask to find out. Heidi wanted him to ask. She should be able to talk about where she'd spent the last two years of her life. Where she was going in just two short months.

"Tell me about them," he said, finally locking eyes with her. His blazed like they always did, like bright blue fire against a dark sky.

"Well, Jenny and Damon live close by. We used to go to church together, and then go to each other's apartments for lunch. Although." She waited as another couple moved past them. "I realize now that we mostly ate pastries for lunch. Pies, and cakes, and turnovers. Whatever we'd been practicing at home."

His fingers squeezed hers. "So you don't always need to eat real food."

"I'll admit I was usually sick on Monday mornings." She

laughed, sucking in the sound when he pulled her closer and slid his arm around her waist.

"I want to hear more," he said, his mouth right at her ear, causing her to shiver in anticipation. "But there's Miss Frannie, and I want you to meet her."

Heidi nodded and put on her most charming smile to meet Frank's mother's best friend.

Heidi didn't think a more perfect weekend could exist. Time with Frank—a lot of time with Frank—and time with her sister, and time to attend church had her feeling peaceful, and happy, and exhausted.

Maggie had left with Chase after church, and Heidi missed her already. The cabin felt too quiet without her in it, and she turned on the radio to fill the silence. Frank had gone to the administration trailer after church, as he'd assigned himself the afternoon chores that Sunday. Heidi had learned that he was fair with his men. They all took rotations on the weekends, so everyone had time off when they wanted or needed it. If that meant he had to haul hay or clean horse stalls, then he did it.

As she began stirring the flour into her butter and water on the double boiler to make *pâte a choux* dough, she thought about Frank and his family. She went through each wrangler she'd come to know.

And she would miss them when it came time for her to leave. But she would be leaving, a decision further cemented by the lesson at church today. Pastor Allan had spoken about sacrifice last month, and this month, he'd moved on to faith. The two things that seemed so dominant in Heidi's life. She knew it wasn't a mistake that she'd moved to Three Rivers, that she was in attendance for those particular sermons.

She finished the dough with a half-cup of finely grated gruyere cheese and spooned the dough into her piping bag. Nothing soothed her as much as a cheese puff—unless she left out the cheese and made cream puffs from the dough. But she'd already put the cheese in all the dough, so cheese puffs it would be.

After swirling them onto her sheet tray and baking them for forty minutes, she let them cool while she leafed through her favorite French pastry cookbook. Her teachers in San Francisco would approve of her golden cheese puffs—but would Frank?

She loaded up a plateful of them and headed for the homestead. Frank had been working on the deck for the past few evenings before the rodeo, but it still didn't look stable enough for her to traipse across. But the new part of the house was framed and walls set. A door had been cut in from the deck, and she'd seen Ben and TJ and Frank use that entrance to the house.

But she didn't dare, not with her delicious cheese puffs at stake. So she went around to the back door, only to find it gone. It had been removed and a bare piece of plywood placed over the opening. An additional frame now jutted from the house on the second floor, and she wondered how big Frank intended this house to be.

She moved back to the side of the house that faced her cabin, where the deck sat. Underneath the deck, Frank had laid pavers for a patio, and she now saw a new entrance there. A fancy new door with a window in the top half. That seemed safer than carrying her precious cheese puffs up the stairs and across rickety decking.

The door opened—she wasn't surprised. She didn't lock her cabin door, and she hadn't used the key ring since that first day, since none of the cowboys locked theirs either. Inside she found a living room with a couch that faced a television set. Two doors stood in front of her, and she could see into a bedroom and a bathroom. Another door to the right showed her the stairs that would lead to the house above.

Another doorway sat at the top, but it was open and she could hear voices filtering down from the kitchen above. At the top of the stairs, the voices manifested as Ben's and Frank's, and Ben's words, "...do about her?" stopped Heidi on the landing, just inside the door.

"I don't know what to do about her," Frank said. "She's leaving the last week of August. School starts in September."

"You gonna ask her to stay?"

"I promised her I wouldn't." Something like a pan hitting the stovetop banged through the house, setting Heidi's already pounding heart into a gallop. Her grip on the plate of cheese puffs increased.

"Well, that was a dumb promise to make."

A few seconds of silence was followed by, "I wasn't in love with her at the time."

Heidi gasped, the sound so loud in the narrowness of the

stairwell. Frank was in love with her? Already?

Everything in her wanted to flee, to get away so she could think things through.

"Maybe tell her that," Ben suggested. "Tell her you love her, and ask her to stay."

"I can't tell her I love her." Frank's footsteps came closer, and Heidi shrank into the wall, praying he wouldn't come all the way to the doorway where she hid. His footsteps retreated, but she still heard him say, "It'll scare her away."

More footsteps came her way, this time from the opposite end of the house. Before Heidi had time to move, or think, or breathe, she came face-to-face with TJ. "Hey," he said. His eyes dropped to the plate she carried. "What are those?"

"Cheese puffs," she said loudly, stepping into the hallway in front of him. "I thought you boys would like them."

He grinned, a hungry look already in his eye. "Maybe I'll just take them back to my room."

But Frank and Ben had heard them, and Frank poked his head around the wall from the kitchen. "Don't you dare let him take them back to his room." His grin didn't look afraid, or sheepish, or embarrassed. He moved down the hall and took the plate from her with one hand and swept the other around her to bring her in for a kiss.

Self-conscious now when she wouldn't have been before she'd heard him admit he loved her, she ended the kiss sooner than she'd done previously. He didn't seem to notice as he towed her away from TJ and down the hall to the barely-functioning kitchen.

Except now it was, in fact, a kitchen. Sure, the floor was still bare plywood covered with cardboard, but new appliances had been installed, and the long island she'd detailed for him had been framed in. The hole for the sink was twice what she had in her cabin, and a space had been left for—"Is that going to be a dishwasher?" She turned toward Frank with hope bouncing through her.

"Yep."

"Frank, this looks amazing." A large living room waited to her right, and the kitchen would easily fit a table for twelve.

"New mudroom around the corner," he said. "It leads to the garage, which I've doubled the size of. Small sitting room in the front, where our living room is now. That goes to the front door."

It was fantastic, all of it. From the new house, to the new yard, to the man putting in all the work. If Heidi's heart didn't feel like it was sitting inside a chest ten sizes too small, she'd have laughed and hugged him for his accomplishments.

Instead, all she could hear was, "I love her," in Frank's voice—and TJ's groan of satisfaction after he stuffed a cheese puff into his mouth.

I love you, Heidi. The words sat in the back of Frank's throat, on the tip of his tongue, ran through his mind while he did payroll, fed calves, hauled hay, built the deck, and trained his horses.

He did not say them. While Heidi laughed with him, brought delicious desserts to his office, told him seemingly everything about herself and her family, and let him kiss her until time had no meaning, she was still planning to leave Three Rivers behind.

Leave *him* behind.

He'd asked her about her remaining classes, her friends in San Francisco, where she lived, went to church, spent her free time. He felt confident he didn't need to worry about another man stealing Heidi away from him.

But he did fret about whether her baking was more important than him. He didn't ask her that, wouldn't ask her to stay when she prepared to move in two weeks. Didn't. Wouldn't. Couldn't.

He twisted the bolt on the radiator and lifted his head out of the engine of the baler. "Okay, try it now."

Matty twisted the starter, and the machine roared to life. Relief sagged through Frank, followed quickly by the knowledge that now he needed to get back out in the fields and get the hay in.

Exhaustion engulfed him. He'd been up until midnight finishing the deck and installing the French doors leading to the kitchen. The flooring had arrived last week, but he hadn't gotten to it yet, because he wanted the exterior finished first. The old siding was coming down next week—he and his brothers would do that—and a brick mason would be coming the following week.

The week Heidi would be leaving.

No matter what Frank thought about, it led to Heidi's departure. Frustrated with himself, he climbed into the tractor, said, "Thanks, Matty. Go see what Terry wants you to do next," and headed out to the hay fields. Some time away from the activity on the ranch would do him some good. At least he hoped it would.

He'd always loved the peacefulness of the range, of the simple act of mowing the hay, of smelling the fresh, country air, of listening to the buzzing of insects. He much preferred being out on the ranch, physically working, but he also understood the necessity of paperwork and keeping files. He thought, though, that one day he could turn most of that over to his general controller.

Frank couldn't believe how quickly July had slipped into history, how fast August was following her. He wanted to lasso time, drag it backward, beg it to slow down. The only way he'd been able to distract himself was through work. He worked from sun up to sun down so he didn't have time to stew before falling asleep at night. If he wasn't running ranch administration, he was physically working on the ranch. If he wasn't training his horses to trust him, come to him, go through the stream a few miles from the main hub of the ranch, he was ordering carpet and choosing paint colors and driving to Amarillo to select furniture for the extra bedrooms, living spaces, and the kitchen in the new, expanded homestead.

As the afternoon wore on, and the rumble of the tractor beneath him lulled him into a relaxed state, Frank enjoyed the sunshine on his bare arms and the slight breeze that kept darting through the cab of the tractor and trying to steal his hat.

He mowed as the sun ducked toward the horizon, as his stomach started to tighten with hunger, as wondered what Heidi had made for dinner.

He wouldn't be the only one to miss her, that was for certain. In the two and a half months she'd been here, she'd captured the heart of every cowhand—or at least their stomachs. No one had a bad word to say about her, and though he'd been paying out the nose for food, it was exactly what he wanted to be spending his money on.

He wondered if he'd be able to replicate what she'd started. Maybe not everyday, but he could put together a decent chili, and he knew how to grill chicken and burgers and hot dogs, and he could lay out sandwich ingredients like a pro.

"You can do that," he said aloud to himself as he rounded the end of the field. "At least a few times a week. You want the familial feeling to remain." And he did, more than anything.

By the time he finished, full darkness had fallen and the headlamp on the tractor cut a path through the night. He made it back to the ranch and parked in the equipment building. His skin itched a bit from all the hay fibers, and he brushed himself off as he headed over to Terry's cabin to let him know what he'd finished.

"You got *all* the fields mowed?" Terry looked as tired as Frank felt. Both men loved ranching, but summer promised so much work and too little time to do it.

"All of 'em."

"Frank," Terry said, his voice a bit chastising.

"It was fine." Frank liked Terry, always had. He'd been working the ranch for two decades, and he knew what he was doing. But Frank wasn't going to tell him why he'd spent so long in the fields tonight. He barely understood why himself.

"I'll get someone out there to bale in the next few days, then."

"Perfect." Frank managed to smile before turning away from the cabin door. His heart rate increased as he approached Heidi's cabin, but her windows sat in darkness. He paused at the bottom of the steps and listened, but he couldn't hear the radio or the hum of the sewing machine he'd given her. He knew she liked to get to bed early since she rose with the sun and started work at the same time as the cowboys. It gave her most of the afternoon to bake and make dinner.

So he continued down the newly shaped lawn to the home that was nearing the completion of its makeover. One of his brothers had left the deck light on for him, and he entered the kitchen to bright lights and blessed air conditioning.

He should do something in the house—the flooring for the kitchen mocked him from the direction of the new mudroom—but he kicked off his boots and pulled open the fridge instead. A container he'd never seen before sat at eye level, with a note attached in Heidi's neat print.

Lasagna night, *she'd written.* Missed you.

"There's bread in the drawer."

Frank glanced at Ben, who leaned against the corner of the wall that led down the hall.

"Thanks." He stuck the lasagna in the microwave, his stomach roaring in displeasure.

"That woman is amazing."

"Ben," Frank warned.

"I'm just sayin'."

"Well, don't."

"Had an interesting conversation with her tonight at dinner."

Frank's heart simultaneously leapt and dropped. He wanted to know everything she'd said, while at the same time it grated that she'd spoken to Ben and not him.

You weren't there, his mind whispered. "Are you gonna tell me about it, or just stand there and gloat?" He yanked open the new bread drawer in the long island and pulled out Heidi's famous garlic bread.

"I rather enjoy the gloating, actually." Ben grinned and folded his arms. "It's fun now that I have something that can get you riled up."

"I'm so glad I can entertain you."

"Seriously, Frank, nothing's ever ruffled you. Our whole lives, I've tried to find something that would make you mad."

"Again," Frank said, piercing his brother with a pointed look. "Not helping."

Ben laughed, and even after he settled into silence, he didn't tell Frank what he'd talked about with Heidi. Determined not to let him know how frustrated Frank felt, he sat at the counter and started eating.

He kept hoping he'd eat something of Heidi's he didn't immediately fall in love with, simply to find something about her that didn't appeal to him. It hadn't happened yet, and it certainly wouldn't with the explosion of tomato and basil in this lasagna.

"It's good, right?" Ben asked, still enjoying himself far too much for Frank's liking.

"Sure is." He flashed Ben a composed grin, as if he wasn't dying a slow death waiting to hear what Heidi had said. He'd seen her that morning for only a few minutes, and the ache to hold her, breathe in the lemony scent of her, kiss her slammed into him like a two-ton bull.

Ben took a piece of bread from the bag and sat next to Frank. "She asked when your birthday was, then asked all kinds of questions about if we had any family traditions surrounding birthdays and what kind of cake you liked best." He bit into the bread and cut a glance at Frank out of the corner of his eye.

"I told her my birthday was on Halloween."

"She didn't seem to know it was the exact day."

Frank frowned and shoveled another spoonful of lasagna into his mouth.

"I told her you were a chocolate fan all day long."

Frank grunted and reached for his own piece of bread. He didn't want to treat Ben badly, but he didn't have a whole lot left in his tank.

"I asked her if she was planning to come visit at Halloween." Ben finished his bread and dusted the crumbs from his mouth. "She suddenly had a lot of work to do, and she left."

The cold spot in Frank's chest that had been expanding all summer shrank the littlest bit. He reminded himself he didn't want her to come visit. He wanted her here with him permanently. He just needed to figure out how to tell her without scaring her into never coming back at all.

After all, a visit was better than nothing.

"Hey, there, beautiful." Frank leaned in the doorway to cabin four, where Heidi held a duster and swiped it along the shelves.

Her face broke into a smile at the sight of him, and he received her into his arms happily. He'd settled on his nickname for her after she confessed to him she didn't like being called sweetheart. Apparently, though, beautiful worked for her, because every time he said it, her cheeks got this gorgeous blush that drove Frank's desire to the stars.

She hugged him tightly, then tipped up on her toes to kiss him. He held her firmly at the waist and enjoyed the taste of her lips, the way she curled her fingers through his hair, knocking his hat clean off his head.

"I missed you last night," he murmured against her mouth.

She put speaking distance between them, much to Frank's disappointment. "Terry kept saying you'd be back any minute, but you never came."

"I wanted to finish all the mowing."

She looked at him with curiosity, almost like she knew there was more to his late return than simply wanting to finish the chores. But she didn't call him on it. Instead, she removed herself from his embrace and picked up his hat. With a sheepish grin, she handed it back to him.

Settling it on his head, he asked, "Go out with me this weekend?"

She picked up her duster and returned to the built-in shelving next to the door. "Sure. What do you have in mind?"

"I need to go to Amarillo and deliver a couple of my trained horses."

A blip of disappointment crossed her expression. "Doesn't sound like something you'd take a girl to do."

"Heidi, I want to meet your parents."

She dropped the duster and stared at him. "You what?"

Disappointment tore through him. "You don't want me to meet them?"

She blinked. Blinked again. "I—"

I love you, Heidi raged through his mind, his bones, his soul. He wanted to meet her father before she left for San Francisco. He'd need to speak with the man about marrying Heidi come spring, and he didn't want that to be the first time they met.

"Ah, I see." He turned away. "I'll go myself. See you later." He made it across the porch and down the steps before he heard any movement from Heidi.

"Frank, wait."

He half-turned back to her, not wanting to give her full view of his heart. He didn't need her to target him there and shoot him straight through the chest.

"I want to go," she said.

"I can deliver the horses, and we can go to lunch," he said, twisting a bit more toward her.

"My mother would love to meet you," she said. "She's been asking me about you for weeks."

That was news to Frank, but he kept the surprise schooled beneath his neutral expression. "So we could go visit them in the afternoon."

"She'll make us dinner," Heidi said. "I'll call her today."

Satisfaction soared through Frank, but he merely gave her a single nod. "All right. See you later." He forced his feet away from her, his nerves running rampant and his mind suddenly focused on what he'd say to her parents when he met them.

Chapter Nine

Heidi woke on Saturday morning earlier than she normally did. It was her second-to-last Saturday in Three Rivers. Next Saturday, Maggie would be here, and they'd load up everything Maggie owned and return to Amarillo.

A drape of sadness settled over her and she took long minutes to admire the cabin that felt like home. She stood at the bedroom window, watching the range beyond the row of cabins. She ran her fingers along the countertop where she'd prepared countless meals and desserts for dozens of men. She sat at the sewing machine Frank had given her, remembering how dear it was to him and how much it had meant that he'd given it to her.

"I don't want to leave this place," she whispered to herself. But over the past couple of months, she'd stuck to the feeling she'd had about finishing school. She'd begged the Lord to tell her if that wasn't what she should do, and He never had. She'd wrestled with Him about why He'd given her Frank at this moment in her life, and she always came back to what Maggie had told her.

She needed to rely on her faith. And she had faith in her and

Frank. She had faith that she was supposed to finish school. She had faith that God would lead her where she needed to be.

"I want to be here," she said louder this time. "Can I come back here?"

God didn't answer, but someone knocked on her door. She recognized Frank's three short raps, and she called, "Come in."

He opened the door and his tall frame filled the entrance, but he didn't come in. Ever the gentleman, he never did. Of course, he didn't seem to have a problem taking her into the barn and kissing her until she couldn't breathe, or sneaking off with her to the remotest side of his house and pressing his lips against hers until she lost the ability to stand.

"Did I hear you say somethin'?" He peered at her with extreme interest.

They'd danced around her leaving for weeks, though he'd questioned her about her courses, her life, her friends in San Francisco.

"No," she said with a smile. "I'm almost ready to go. Just need shoes." She scampered into the bedroom so she wouldn't have to exist under the weight of his stare. She pulled on sandals and returned to the front room.

Frank had entered her cabin and closed the door behind him. She froze one step outside her bedroom, her hands fiddling with her hair. She lowered them to her sides at the intense look on his face.

"Heidi, I heard you ask if you could come back here." He held completely still, his voice low and even.

"I was just talkin' to myself." She tried for a giggle, but it came out strangled and she cut it off immediately.

"I want you to come back here," he said. His seriousness endeared him more to her, and her heart warmed. "Do you want to come back here?"

"Yes," she whispered.

She expected him to stride toward her, sweep her into his arms, profess his love for her. Though she'd heard him tell his brother that he loved her almost two months ago, he'd never said the words to her.

He stayed right where he was, his blue eyes sparking from across the room. "Do you know why I want to meet your parents?"

She'd been speculating to herself, even mentioned it to Maggie during their phone call the previous night. Maggie had said their mother was planning a feast and she'd warned all the girls—and Daddy—to be on their best behavior. A tremor ran through Heidi when she said, "No."

"I want to meet them now so when I go to ask your father if I can marry you, that it won't be the first time they've seen me."

The air rushed out of the cabin, and though Heidi gasped, she got no oxygen. The supreme confidence with which Frank delivered his words made Heidi admire him even more. In that moment, she knew without a shadow of a doubt that she was in love with Frank Ackerman.

"Frank, what are you saying?"

He moved, finally. Came around the couch, his eyes never leaving hers. He took both her hands in his. "I'm sayin' I love you,

Heidi. I want to marry you someday."

Warmth filled her like a balloon, and fireworks popped in her head. "Someday?"

"After you finish school." He dipped his head closer to her ear. "Do you think you might want to do that once you finish school?" He traced his lips down her earlobe, and pressed them to the soft spot on her neck just below her jawbone.

She shivered, and instead of telling him she loved him too, or that yes, she'd like to marry him once she finished school, she brought her mouth to his, hoping her kiss could say everything her voice couldn't.

Nerves assaulted Heidi as Frank neared her parents' home. Lunch had been romantic and perfect, the exact personification of Frank. She knew Maggie wouldn't be a problem, and she wondered if Bridgette would even be home. Kayla, the youngest, probably wouldn't do much more than goggle at Frank.

Please let Daddy like him, she prayed as Frank turned right and her house came into view.

"Third one on the right," she said.

He pulled alongside the curb since he had the horse trailer hooked to his truck, and put the vehicle in park.

"I'm so nervous," Heidi admitted.

"You bring home boyfriends a lot?" he asked.

She rolled her eyes at him. "You know the answer to that."

"So I'm the first?" He wiped his hands on his jeans.

"The very first," she confirmed, her eye on the front door. She hoped Maggie would keep everyone inside until they came to the door. She'd promised she would. Heidi was grateful for a friend and sister like Maggie. "Should we go, then?"

"What if they don't like me?" Frank's voice ghosted through the cab, the first time Heidi had ever seen anything but pure confidence from the man.

"That would be impossible," she assured him, though she wondered if Daddy would ever like any of the men she or her sisters brought home. He'd never liked any of Maggie's boyfriends.

She leaned over and kissed his cheek. "Come on." She nudged him toward his door. "You gotta get out, cowboy."

He gazed at her with pure love in his eyes and gave her a chaste kiss on the lips. "All right, then." He slid out and when she joined him, he took her hand in his.

Her heart pounded as they mounted the steps and she knocked twice before pushing open the door. "Hello," she called.

"They're here!" Maggie called and she appeared in the doorway a moment later, a huge smile on her face. "Hey, guys." She came forward and hugged Heidi, then pulled Frank into a hug too. Surprise etched on his face, but he went with it. When he straightened, both her parents stood in the doorway leading to the kitchen and the rest of the house.

"Hey, Momma." Heidi moved forward and hugged her mom and daddy hello. She turned back to Frank, her throat so, so dry. But seeing him standing there in his sexy jeans and blue polo, that cowboy hat on his head and those old boots on his feet, she grinned with happiness. "Momma and Daddy, this is my boyfriend, Frank Ackerman."

He swept forward and shook her father's hand and gave her mother a peck on the cheek. His deep voice filled the house, and his infectious laugher had them all smiling within a few minutes. Heidi stood next to Maggie, who elbowed her and gave her the widest smile and two thumbs up.

Heidi should've known Frank would charm everyone. After all, he'd captivated her within seconds. Even Daddy seemed under Frank's spell, and he asked Frank to come into the backyard and help him grill the chicken.

Frank went without a backward glance, already asking his father questions about the feed store.

"Holy brown cows, Heidi," Kayla said once the back door had slammed shut. "He's gorgeous."

"Kayla," their mother said, but she moved to the kitchen window and peered out it to where the two men stood by the grill.

"Did you see him, Mom?"

"He's very handsome," Maggie said. "I told you he was."

"He's handsome all right," Momma said. "He's a cowboy?" She finally tore her gaze from the backyard.

"He owns the ranch where I've been working," Heidi said.

"He owns the ranch?" Momma pulled out an onion and began slicing it. "Set the stove, Kayla."

"Yeah," Heidi said as Kayla turned on the gas and set a pan on the burner. She added a dollop of butter and went back to staring out the window. Momma dumped the onions in the pan and added salt and pepper.

"Things are serious?" Momma asked, the first of her million-question strategy.

Heidi exchanged a glance with Maggie, and decided to go with full disclosure. "When he came to pick me up this morning, we talked about getting married."

Momma's hand flinched as she stirred the onions. "When will that happen?"

"I don't know, Momma. I'm gonna finish school first." Heidi's joviality faded a little and she too moved to the kitchen window so she could see Frank. Eight months had never felt so long, so much like a life sentence.

The following Saturday, Frank arrived at Heidi's by daybreak. She and Maggie would be up early to load the truck and head back to Amarillo. Heidi had a flight to San Francisco that evening.

He'd done everything he could over the past week to shower her with love and affection. She knew how he felt about her, but the chasm in his chest deepened with each day that he told her he loved her and she didn't say it back.

He'd enjoyed meeting her family, and they genuinely seemed to like him. Heidi had shown up at his place after church the next day, claiming that he was all her family had talked about for a solid day. If Maggie was to be believed, and though the woman had a streak for the dramatic, Frank didn't think she'd lie.

He settled on Heidi's front step to wait for the first sign of movement. He didn't want either woman to carry anything heavier than their purse. If he couldn't get Heidi to stay, he was going to make leaving easy so she'd want to return.

"You can't ask her to stay," he told himself, same as he had been for the past week. He'd been surprised at his own boldness last week, tellin' her he loved her and askin' her if she'd come back to him. He'd told himself for a solid month not to tell her, and yet he had.

It had felt so good to say those three words. To see the shock and reciprocated love in her face.

"She didn't say it back," he reminded himself, and then he wondered why he needed her to. Her love for him was plain to see in her expression, obvious to him in her touch, clear as day in her actions. And yet, he found he needed to hear it declared in her pretty little voice.

Gravel crunched under boots, and Frank looked up to see Chase coming down the path. "Mornin'," he said.

"Hey." Chase settled on the step with Frank. "How're you holdin' up?"

"Fine," Frank said. "Just fine." He hadn't discussed his personal relationship with anyone but Ben and TJ, though Chase knew the most out of any of his men. "You?"

"My girlfriend ain't moving halfway across the country."

"But she lives an hour away. You've done the long-distance thing, at least a little."

"Yeah, I guess. I just call her when I can, and send her letters, and ask her to come meet me in town."

Meeting with Heidi would be out, unless Frank wanted to fly to San Francisco. *You could do that*,d he thought for the first time. He had good men on the ranch. A capable general controller, a reliable foreman. Even with his brothers leaving next week, he could take a weekend and go see the ocean if he wanted to.

"Heard a rumor going around town," Chase said. "They're saying an Ackerman bought a diamond ring."

"Ah, that would be Ben," Frank said with a smile. "He's gonna propose to Becca before he goes back to school."

Chase nodded, turning when noise came from the cabin behind them. "Sounds like they're up."

"You go," Frank said, and Chase got up to knock on the door. Maggie opened it and giggled when she saw him. He leaned down and kissed her before entering the cabin.

"You coming in?" she asked Frank, but he shook his head.

"Let me know when you're ready to load up," he said.

"I'll send Heidi out."

"You don't need—" But Maggie had already turned into the house and called for her sister. Heidi came out a few minutes later and sat next to him on the step.

Everything in him wanted to reach for her hand, lace his fingers through hers, turn and press a loving kiss to her temple. But a rush of apprehension, of anger, of alarm raced through him. He couldn't touch her. Couldn't speak.

She snuggled into his side and laid her head against his bicep. "I'll call you tomorrow night, right?"

"Right," he managed to scrape out of his throat.

The country silence seemed so loud, something Frank had never experienced. The muted sounds of Chase and Maggie's voice from inside the house brought the only sound.

He finally relented to his urge to hold her hand and reached for her. The tension between them evaporated like dew in the summer sun, and she leaned farther into him until he lifted his arm around her and cradled her against his chest. "I'm gonna miss you, beautiful." His voice sounded unlike him, thick with longing and love.

"I know," she said. "I'll miss you too."

He tilted his body toward her to kiss her, taking his time and holding on to each touch of their lips a little longer. "I love you," he whispered against her mouth, holding himself back so she could say it before he kissed her again.

She didn't, and Frank felt like he was falling for a few long moments. Then he stood and cleared his throat. "So, you all packed up? What do you need help with this morning?"

She directed him to the pile of boxes just inside the door. The way they were taped and labeled screamed of her organizational skills and he smiled at just how Heidi she was. The cabin sparkled, as if she and Maggie had spent all night cleaning it.

Chase and Maggie sat at the kitchen table, their hands intertwined on the tabletop as they spoke in low voices. Frank steeled himself and picked up the first box. Then it was just a matter of putting one foot in front of the other, enduring simple conversation, and kissing Heidi good-bye one last time.

Then she climbed into the truck with her sister, waved at him, and left.

He watched the truck round the bend, kicking up dust as it went. Chase clapped him on the shoulder and headed back toward the cabins. But Frank stood in the parking lot until every dust particle had settled, his heart shrinking and the well of regret deepening with every passing moment.

"She's gone," he said, and the harshness in his voice startled him. But she was gone, and she hadn't told Frank she loved him, and he stomped back to the homestead, furious with himself for saying things he shouldn't have said, making promises he shouldn't have made, falling in love with a woman he'd known wouldn't stay for more than a summer.

Dear Heidi,

Frank stared at the piece of paper, writing never really his strong suit. He didn't know what to say. He couldn't tell her of his foul mood. Wouldn't tell her that he'd finished the tile in the kitchen yesterday, and the carpet had been laid in the living room and all the bedrooms. In fact, the house—without her—felt like a colossal waste of time and money.

He didn't want to burden her with his darkness, didn't want her to think he spent days on end staring out the window onto the range, as if he'd see her driving back to greet him. The window faced in the opposite direction, and yet he pictured her leaning in his office doorway, that youthful sparkle in her eyes and a plate of something delicious in her hand.

And he wasn't the only one with a grumpy face and a growly voice. Most of his men wore frowns and kept their heads down, getting the job done before they escaped back to the solace of their cabins.

A week passed after this fashion, then two. Frank left his office one Friday afternoon, intending to put on the TCU football game and order in a pizza or two. As he passed Heidi's cabin, an idea bloomed in his mind.

He wouldn't just order one or two pizzas, and he wouldn't watch the game alone. He'd invite all his men to come to the expanded homestead to eat and socialize and watch. He'd thought about providing dinner a few times a week, but he'd been so focused on trying to fill the hole Heidi had left in his life, that he hadn't done anything yet.

Pivoting, he went back to the administration trailer, hoping Terry hadn't left yet. A quick check of his watch, and Frank thought he'd find him behind the desk. Sure enough, Terry still sat just inside the door. He glanced up when Frank entered.

"Boss?"

Frank ignored the surprise and interest in Terry's voice. "As the men come in, will you let them know I'll have pizza at my place tonight? TCU is playing on TV in a couple of hours, and anyone's welcome to come eat and watch."

Terry blinked a couple of times as a slow smile spread across his face. "I'll let everyone know."

A flash of...something moved through Frank's body. It took

him a few minutes to figure out what it was, as he hadn't felt anything but gloom and despair in the two weeks since Heidi had left.

But now he felt satisfied—good, almost. Like he could do what she'd done. Sure, he'd be a poor substitute for Heidi—her warmth, her cooking, the way she looked at everyone like they had a mountain of potential—but he could try.

"Boss?" Terry asked again.

"Yeah?" Frank blinked and focused on his general controller.

"I've been thinkin' about something."

A tremor shot through Frank's body, his recent euphoria gone. "What is it?"

Terry glanced toward the open area where the cowboys gathered for their morning assignments. He met Frank's eye again. "I think it's time for me to go back to Peach Valley."

Frank took the news into his mind, rolled it around for a few moments. "Everything okay with your family?"

"My parents are getting older," Terry admitted. "And my wife would like to be closer to her sister too."

Frank cleared his throat. "Yeah, of course." He too looked down the hall to the empty area. "When do you think you'll go?"

"Not until the end of the year," Terry said. "That should give you time to hire a new general controller, and I can train 'em up right."

Relief washed through Frank. He could find a good general controller in five months. With his brothers gone, his father had mentioned moving out sooner as well, leaving Frank to run the ranch a few months earlier than he'd anticipated.

"That should work," Frank said, sounding more sure than he felt. He shook Terry's hand, ducked his head, and left the admin trailer.

"You can do this," he coached himself as he passed Heidi's cabin again and crossed the lawn to the now-bricked house. With Ben and TJ gone, the homestead seemed ridiculously huge. But his father could get around easier, and it was a place Frank could invite all his men and have them fit.

"Dad," he called as he entered the house from the new deck. "I'm ordering pizza for the game. You want to go into town with me to pick it up?"

His father's favored chair in the now-formal sitting room squeaked, and a few moments later, he appeared in the kitchen. "Sure." Frank didn't know how much his dad knew about his relationship with Heidi. He'd always been open with his sons, and he had bought the engagement ring Ben had given to Becca the Sunday night Heidi had called for the first time.

They'd packed up the next week and gone to Dallas so he could finish dental school, and Frank had heard rumors around the ranch and town of their spring wedding. Jealousy had consumed him for a day or two, and a jolt of it hit him now as he grabbed the phone to dial into Papa Henry's, the only pizza joint in Three Rivers.

He pushed away the negative feeling. Tonight was about continuing what Heidi had started, and he wasn't going to waste any more time with negativity.

Chapter Ten

After the first couple of weeks, Frank wrote every week, like clockwork. If Heidi didn't get a letter on Wednesday afternoon, she'd know something was wrong. She smiled at the slant of his print, and loved feeling like she still lived on the ranch, entertaining the cowhands in the evenings and watching the sun go down with Frank's hand in hers.

He told her of prepping the fields for winter, and sealing the horse barn, and finishing the homestead. She longed for the easier days of summer, but she focused on her baking, pushing herself to do better everyday. After all, she hadn't left Frank behind in Three Rivers simply to pine over him.

She baked her way through September and half of October, hanging on for Sunday evenings when he would call and she could hear the deep timbre of his voice, and Wednesdays when she could imagine that voice through his words.

His birthday was coming up, and she was determined to see him on Halloween. Physically be in the same space as him, kiss him, and maybe even be brave enough to tell him she loved him. If she had one regret about leaving Three Rivers Ranch, it was that she'd done it without telling him how much she cared about him.

"Melanie," she said on the Monday morning before Halloween, which miracle of miracles, fell on a Saturday. "I need to talk to you about taking a day off."

Her instructor looked up from the notes on her desk. "Heidi," she said warmly, a smile springing to her face. "Come on in." She rose halfway out of her seat. "Just slide those cookbooks onto the floor."

Heidi cleared the chair and sat down. "My boyfriend's birthday is on Saturday, and I want to go see him in Texas." She braided her fingers together and pulled them apart. "I was wondering if I could be excused from class on Monday so I could travel back that day."

Absences were rare in the pastry program. Heidi had only ever seen students miss for extreme sickness. She waited while Melanie appraised her. "How many days have you missed in your program?" she asked.

"None." Heidi had been blessed with extremely good health.

"Then I don't see why you can't take this one day." Melanie smiled. "But you'll have to make up the baking hours. You need four hundred by December fifteenth."

"Of course," Heidi said, relief and gratitude streaming through her with the speed of a jet plane. Making Frank's chocolate birthday cake would certainly count. She left Melanie's office and went straight to the bank of phones in the student lounge. After calling the airline and arranging a flight that would get her home late Friday night, she dialed Maggie to tell her the good news and to ask her to buy the ingredients Heidi needed to make the perfect birthday cake for Frank.

When she got to class, Melanie already stood at the front, but she hadn't started yet. Heidi barely had time to pull on her chef's coat before Melanie said, "Today, we tackle one of the hardest pastries to make: a soufflé. It's not time consuming. It's not difficult. But it is delicate and temperamental, and even the most experienced bakery chefs avoid them." She beamed at them. "And we'll be doing a chocolate soufflé today, and it will be an item on your final cooking challenge at the end of the term."

Heidi pushed Frank and thoughts of her visit with him in just five short days to the back of her mind. She watched, took notes, read through recipes. Then she tried her hand at her own soufflé.

Once hers was in the oven, she cleaned up her station and sat at the counter to read through the science behind the soufflé. Someone sat next to her, and she glanced up to find Damon there. She smiled at him. "Hey, how's the soufflé going?"

"In the oven." He returned her smile. "I wanted to talk to you about something."

Heidi paused in her studies and focused on him. "What is it?"

"I'm looking for a partner to start my bakery." He spoke slowly and clearly, one thing about Damon Heidi had always liked. He went to church with her too, and they'd spent a lot of time together on Sunday afternoons. He had light brown hair and dark brown eyes. And as he outlined why he wanted a partner, where he thought he'd open his bakery, and how he'd come to decide to ask Heidi, his enthusiasm grew.

"So, I'm wondering if you want to be my partner," he finished.

"I don't need an answer right away. Think about it. Let me know." He started to stand, but Heidi put her hand on his arm.

"You said you already have funding?"

"My father is a bank manager," he said. "But I want a partner. Someone to collaborate with in the recipes, someone to share the responsibility with. You're detailed, and organized, and well, Heidi, everyone knows you're the best pastry chef here." He beamed at her. "Like I said, I don't need an answer right now." He walked away, leaving Heidi with more questions than answers.

She'd often wondered how she'd get up at three a.m. and run a bakery alone. She'd taken classes in business management and finance, and having a partner was something that had been discussed in detail. They even had sample partnership documents. And here stood Damon, asking her to become his partner. And he already had financing.

She felt numb, frozen, and her mind could only scream one thing: *What about Frank?*

By the time Heidi arrived back in Texas, her nerves felt like she'd put them through a lawnmower. She'd slept little that week as she tried to figure out what to do. Should she even go home for Frank's birthday if she wasn't planning on returning to Three Rivers next spring? Damon wanted to stay right in San Francisco and open his bakery. He'd grown up there, and his father's bank was there.

She'd tried to soothe herself by practicing Frank's cake in the evenings, and she'd eaten most of her experiments. And she'd spent long hours on her knees, trying to figure out what God wanted her to do.

It always came back to the same question—why was He giving her these opportunities if she wasn't supposed to take them? And if she wasn't, could He please give her the strength to know what to say, what to do?

She'd felt His presence near, but no definitive answers had come. So she stuck to her plan of going home and visiting Frank for his birthday. With the help of Chase, she'd managed to keep it a surprise. He'd make sure Frank was home in the morning, and though it was nearly midnight by the time Heidi arrived at her parents' house, she started the chocolate cake. It would need time to cool before she could frost it, and she didn't want to waste her limited time with Frank tomorrow by baking.

Maggie kept her company in the kitchen, asking question after question about San Francisco and talking a mile a minute about Chase and everything that had happened in the past two months. Heidi had called her religiously, something she knew her sister needed. But there was something about being together that couldn't be achieved over a phone line.

Finally, Maggie got to Frank. "So you obviously still like him."

Heidi added half of the flour to the cake mixture and stirred. "Obviously."

"You guys been talking about marriage anymore?"

Heidi shook her head, not trusting her voice to stay even if she spoke.

"Do you want to marry him?"

Such easy questions, and yet so many factors complicated what she wanted. She added another egg, stirred, and then put in the rest of the flour mixture. With the batter done, she faced her sister. "I love him, but I haven't told him yet."

Maggie's eyes widened. "Why not?"

Heidi scraped the batter into her prepared pans. "I was scared to tell him before I left, and then it didn't seem like something I should say over the phone or in a letter." She slid the cakes into the oven.

"Well, you'll tell him tomorrow," Maggie said matter-of-factly, like that problem could be solved so easily.

"There's something else."

"What?"

"A friend of mine has asked me to partner with him to open a bakery in San Francisco."

Maggie stared at her. Heidi couldn't tell what she was thinking, but she didn't like the weight of her sister's eyes. "I'm going to talk to Frank about it."

"What for?" Maggie asked. "He's not going to move to San Francisco, Heidi. He *owns* the *biggest* ranch in the *Texas* Panhandle."

Heidi collapsed at the bar with her sister. "I know."

"You can't tell him about the bakery," Maggie insisted. "And I hate to say it, but you probably shouldn't tell him you love him if you're going to choose a bakery over him."

"I don't know what to do." Heidi wanted Maggie to tell her she'd figure it out. But when her sister remained quiet, that silence said it all.

She woke early the next morning to frost the cake and get out to the ranch before too much of the day slipped away. Her mother met her in the kitchen with a smile and a hug. After Maggie's judgment, Heidi sank into her mother's arms, and wept.

"What's wrong?" Her mother stroked her hair and kept her close.

Heidi couldn't answer, so she just took comfort from her mother, the way she had as a child and things had gone wrong.

"Is it Frank?"

As if hit by lightning, Heidi realized that the problem was *absolutely not Frank*.

It was her.

Her and her dreams of owning a bakery. She pulled away from her mother and wiped her face before donning an apron. As she mixed cream cheese and butter, chocolate and powdered sugar, she told her mother everything.

"And I just don't know what to do." Heidi paused in her work and met her mom's eye. "How did you know to marry Daddy?"

"I loved him," Momma said simply. "I loved him so much, I wanted to be with him forever." She covered Heidi's hand with one of hers. "I see that you love Frank that way too."

"Then why is this so hard?" Heidi reached for her cake decorating kit and filled a pastry bag with frosting.

"Sometimes we have to struggle through things before they become clear."

Heidi felt like she'd been swimming upstream since the day she met Frank. Maybe being with him was too hard. Maybe she didn't love him as much as she needed to. As always, *Bakery or Frank?* rolled through her mind on an endless loop. Thankfully, she didn't need to concentrate as hard as usual to produce a beautifully decorated cake.

She drove alone to Three Rivers Ranch for the first time, her knuckles white against the steering wheel. She couldn't understand why her nerves were rioting, or why it suddenly seemed like a very bad idea to show up on Frank's front porch unannounced.

But she forced herself onward, down the dirt road and around the bend. She pulled into his driveway and put the truck in park as she marveled at the transformation of the homestead. The house now had dark brick, and it loomed on the property like a heavy presence.

"Just like Frank," she said to herself. Taking a deep breath, she collected the cake from its spot next to her and got out of the truck. She made it up the steps to the front door but hadn't knocked before someone opened it.

Frank stood there in all his glory, wearing his cowboy hat and boots, those intoxicating jeans, and a blue and white plaid shirt. The short sleeves showed off his muscles, and Heidi remembered all the reasons she loved him.

"Happy birthday." She thrust the cake toward him. "I was told chocolate is your favorite."

He took the cake and turned back to the house. His silence did little to ease her discomfort. She wasn't sure if she should follow him or just get back in the truck and go. He returned, cakeless, a moment later, his gaze raking from the top of her head to the soles of her feet.

They reached for each other in the same breath, and Heidi's fears evaporated with his touch. With the way his strong hands cradled her face, slid across her shoulders and down her back. "Heidi," he murmured just before he brought his lips to hers.

She melted into his embrace, relieved that the confusion and anxiety that seemed to assault her from every side couldn't penetrate the circle of his arms. She wanted to stay with him forever, and she wondered if this was the feeling Momma had spoken of.

Heidi broke the kiss, barely removing her mouth from his. "I love you, Frank. I wanted to see you on your birthday."

He pulled further back, his eyes searching, searching, searching hers. "You love me?"

"I love you." Looking into the electricity of his eyes, she realized the words were important, knew he'd wanted her to say them before she'd left, knew she'd hurt him when she didn't. "I'm sorry I didn't tell you earlier."

"It's fine." He brushed his lips against hers for a microsecond, a tease.

"It's not fine. I didn't know how much you needed to hear me say I loved you."

He moved his mouth to her neck as she spoke, and though the morning air definitely held a fall chill, Heidi felt hot from head to toe. She held onto his broad shoulders for dear life, like she was drowning and only he could save her.

"You've said it now." The rumble of his voice sent shock waves through her, and a happiness like she'd never known infused itself into her soul.

"Maybe we should go inside," she suggested as his hands crept up her back and his lips traced a path along her earlobe.

He stepped back and chuckled, securing her hand in his. "Good idea. You can see the completely remodeled homestead." He led her into the house, but they didn't make it out of the formal living room before Frank wrapped her in his arms again, and kissed her, kissed her, kissed her like he was a dying man and she his savior.

Frank watched Heidi slice into his birthday cake, still somewhat shocked she was here. In the flesh, *here* at Three Rivers Ranch. Joy like he'd never known had engulfed him at the sight of her. And kissing her? Felt like the first time all over again.

When he'd heard someone pull into his driveway, he'd checked out the window, but couldn't see who it was until she slid from the cab. His heart had catapulted to the top of his skull, and it still pounded there, breathless, anxious to hold her close and ask her about everything.

She slid him a large slice of cake, along with a flirtatious smile. It took all his willpower to pick up his fork instead of lunging for her and kissing her again. He took a bite of the cake, and his eyes rolled back in his head. "Heidi, I don't see how you have anything left to learn at pastry school."

She giggled as she slid onto the barstool next to him. "Thank you." She leaned on his arm and rested her face against his bicep. "I'm glad you like it."

He swallowed another bite, and tipped his chin toward her. "I like you."

Her smile came instantly, and Frank abandoned his treat in favor of her lips. After he finished his cake, he settled onto the couch with Heidi tucked into his side and flipped on the television with the remote control.

It was football season, and he'd planned to spend the morning working and the afternoon, well, working on the house with a football game in the background. Now, though, he couldn't seem to concentrate on anything but Heidi, which seemed to suit her just fine.

"Tell me about school," he said after twenty minutes of kissing her.

"It's school," she said. "Up early and in classes most of the day."

"You goin' home tomorrow?"

"Monday," she said. "I wanted to spend the whole weekend with you. I saw a sign on the way in about a Halloween parade?"

"Yeah, it's tonight," he said. "It's usually for little kids, but they have a chili cook-off and a trunk decorating contest. Then you can send your littles down the row of cars to go trick-or-treating."

"You don't sound like you were planning to go."

"I wasn't." He pulled back and peered down at her. "You want to go?"

"I like chili."

"I can make chili," he said. "In fact, I need to get started on that.

I've invited the boys over for dinner tonight." He slipped out from under her and headed into the kitchen. She knelt on the couch and put her arms on the back of it as she watched him.

"You can make chili?"

"Sure." He set a cast iron skillet on the stove and turned on the flame. "I mean, it's not Heidi Duffin level, but it'll feed everyone well enough."

She cocked her head to the side as he put a couple of pounds of ground chuck into the pan and pulled an onion from the bowl beside the fridge. "You been feedin' everyone?"

His lips quirked up at the country twang in her voice. "A couple of times a week." He shrugged. "We're gettin' by." His voice took on a haunted quality on the last sentence, and he swallowed to tame it back into normalcy. He didn't want her to know how hard things had been without her. How lonely he was, especially with his brothers—and now his father—gone too. How he ached to have her here with him, filling this house with the love and joy that would make it a home.

"You want to make cornbread to go with it?" He glanced up at her after he dumped the onions into the pan with the beef.

"Sure." She joined him in the kitchen, and the intoxicating scent of her perfume called to him to take her back to the couch and kiss her some more. Instead, he focused on the peppers, and the beans, and the seasonings. He wanted to show her that he could put together dinner, not only for himself, but for her, and all his cowboys.

He wanted to prove to her that he'd take care of her, that she could be happy here at Three Rivers Ranch. He stirred his chili and set the heat on low so it could simmer. She finished her dough and slid it into the oven. "Thirty minutes," she said.

"Long enough to take a tour of the house," he said. "I think you'll like it." This time, he tucked her hand in his and led her down the hall, where he'd put three bedrooms, a master bathroom, and another bathroom. It flowed around the stairs that led down to the basement, and ended back in the living room where the TV still broadcast the game.

"This is my bedroom," he said, barely pausing long enough for her to look inside. "These are guest bedrooms."

"Looks like they're for Daisy and Duke." She stared at the dog beds along the wall.

"They like being in the house better than the barn." He didn't want to tell her that he needed the dogs nearby. That they soothed him, made the house fell less empty, even if all they did was sleep here.

What he really wanted to say was these bedrooms were for his kids—her kids—the kids he wanted to have with her. He clamped his mouth shut and continued the tour. It had taken her months to tell him she loved him. He wasn't going to bring up children on their first weekend together since August.

"Your father moved out?"

"Last week." Frank steered her past the bedrooms and bathroom and back to the couch so he could kiss her again.

"What about the basement?" She giggled as he placed a kiss on her throat.

"I'll show you later," he said, unwilling to lose even a second of time with Heidi.

Waking to the scent of honey and baking bread reminded Frank of who had come to visit him. He sat up in bed and rubbed his face, then scrubbed his fingers through his hair. Heidi had stayed in her old cabin, and she'd promised she'd be back to make him a birthday breakfast.

After feeding all the cowboys and entertaining them for a few hours, he and Heidi had snuggled together on the couch until almost midnight. He didn't think he'd ever tire of kissing her, of running his fingers through her honeyed hair, or looking into those intoxicating eyes. She'd told him about her instructor, her upcoming finals, and how she was missing several hours of required baking time to visit him. Then she'd said she'd make up some of the time by coming over early to make breakfast.

He pulled on a shirt and stepped into the hallway. Heidi hummed as she worked in the kitchen, and Frank made his steps light as he approached the doorway. He leaned against the wall and watched her work, cutting butter into flour and then adding milk to make biscuits.

Something that looked suspiciously like homemade jam sat on the counter top, and when she turned to check the oven, she caught his eye. "Snooping?"

He chuckled and gathered her into his arms for a good morning kiss. "Just watching." She wore pajamas and a pair of sandals. "You goin' to church with me?"

"Yes," she said. "I just wanted to get these in before you woke. I know how you like to get up early."

"It's not that I like it," he said, keeping her close and swaying to non-existent music. "It's just what happens. Habit."

An hour later, fully stuffed with the flakiest and butteriest biscuits he'd ever eaten, he stepped into the shower. Heidi had just left to get ready, and Frank wondered what Pastor Allan would say today, it being a new month and all. He'd been choosing topics and sticking to them for the past several months, and today marked the beginning of November.

He slid into a row near the middle of the congregation, his hand wound tightly around Heidi's, just as it had been for the past hour since he'd picked her up at her cabin. He made easy conversation with the family next to him, glad when the pastor finally stood up to start the meeting.

"One of the Lord's commandments is to be honest. In the Bible, it says, 'Thou shalt not bear false witness.' We must learn to tell the truth in an ever-increasing society where deceit seems to be rewarded."

Heidi's hand on his tightened to the point of pain, and he glanced down at her. She stared at Pastor Allan, her face draining of all color. "Hey." Frank leaned over and whispered to her. "You okay?"

She startled, released his hand, and looked at him. "Yes. Sorry."

"God is truth," Pastor Alan continued. "He is honesty. We must learn to be honest with ourselves, with others, and with God."

Frank enjoyed the sermon, though he kept getting distracted by the presence of Heidi next to him every time she shifted. Or her scent would suddenly penetrate his senses, and he'd tune out while he argued with himself about doing more than holding her hand in church. By the end of the sermon, Frank felt stretched thin, and he hurried Heidi to his truck and back to the ranch.

He'd planned to feed everyone sandwiches, and she helped him set everything out before heading over to her cabin to change. She didn't come back when everyone else did, but Frank didn't worry too much about it. Maybe she needed a few minutes alone. Maybe she wanted to call her sister.

She came back just as the last cowboy started putting food on his plate, and the place turned into choruses of, "Afternoon, Miss Heidi," and "So good to see you back at the ranch, Miss Heidi," and Frank cringed when he heard someone ask, "When you comin' back for good, Miss Heidi?"

He heard her laughter, but not her answer, and by the time he met her eye, the conversation had moved on to something else. He loitered near the refrigerator, not eating. He wanted his men to have all they wanted, be comfortable in his home. They sat at two long tables he'd set up in the kitchen because of the nasty wind this afternoon.

He finally went through the line and built his own sandwich, finding a spot next to Heidi at the bar.

"Thanks for lunch, Frank." She grinned at him and bit into her sandwich.

He wanted to point out how he'd purchased everything—no

actual cooking involved—but said, "Thanks," instead. Frank wanted the cowboys there, but with Heidi in the room too, he just wanted them gone.

They seemed to be able to pick up on his mood, and everyone cleared out before too long. He yawned as he started cleaning up lunch. "Wow, I'm tired."

"Kept you up too late, did I?" She flashed him a flirtatious smile, but it didn't quite sit right on her face. Something was wrong, but she was working hard to cover it up. He let her, hoping she'd bring it up on her own.

They cleaned up together, and Frank turned the TV on low and settled into the couch. "I might fall asleep," he warned her. "I often do on Sunday afternoons."

"It is a very relaxing time," she said as she sat next to him.

He handed her the remote control. "You can put it on anything you want."

"This is fine."

"This is the NFL." He cocked his right eyebrow at her.

"I don't mind."

She didn't seem to be watching the TV. She faced it, yes, but her expression suggested she was somewhere else, thinking about something else.

"So something interesting happened this week," she said. She wouldn't look at him, and her voice came out a bit high, a bit strained.

"Tell me about it." He closed his eyes and tried to ignore the panic rushing into his body. Didn't work, and his heartbeat sounded as if it existed in his eardrums.

"You remember me telling you about Damon? That friend of mine I go to church with?"

Frank suddenly felt like the ground had turned to ice. Slippery and cracked, and like it couldn't bear his weight. "Yeah."

"He asked me to be his partner," Heidi said. "For a bakery he has funding for in San Francisco."

Frank's eyes snapped open at the same time his heart plummeted to the basement. He stared at Heidi, trying to figure out why she'd brought this up now. He couldn't decide if she wanted the partnership or not. Couldn't tell how she felt just by looking at her.

"And?" he prompted.

"And I'm thinking about it."

The words broke Frank, and he pushed himself into a sitting position. Fury flowed through him with the strength of water gushing over a cliff, and he tried to push it back, contain it. But he'd been damming his feelings for far too long, and words pushed, pushed, pushed against the back of his throat.

He'd never been one to speak in anger, so he got up and left her sitting there on his couch.

"Frank?" she called after him.

"Be right back," he said, hurrying to his bedroom and closing the door. He leaned against it, his chest heaving. He knew what he wanted to tell her about the bakery partnership. He wanted to tell her to forget about it. To move back tomorrow. To marry him that next weekend and move into the homestead and never leave him again.

Why doesn't she want any of that? Pure desperation pulled through him, stitched him tight with anxiety. His stomach turned, and he swallowed against the sick feeling. *What do I do?*

Tell her the truth.

He wasn't sure if it was God or Pastor Allan whose voice had come into his mind, but Frank knew what he had to do. He took a breath to calm himself and opened the door. But he felt anything but calm as he moved down the hall and into the kitchen. She sat in the same place on the couch where he'd left her.

He sat next to her, all the lessons and sermons he'd heard over the past several months crowding into his brain at the same time. "Heidi, I need to tell you something."

She brought her gaze to his face, but he kept his attention on the floor. "I need to be honest with you. I can't keep doin' this. I'm not cut out for long distance relationships. I love you, and I want you here all the time."

She sucked in a breath but didn't speak. Frank continued, "So I'll make it real easy for you. I can see I'm holding you back, and that's the last thing I want. I don't want to be in the way of what you've dreamt about your whole life."

Her hand landed lightly on his forearm, a brand he'd feel all his days. "What are you saying?"

"I'm saying I think we should be done, Heidi. I won't write you; you won't write me back. You do your bakery, and I'll run my ranch." His voice came out strained, and everything inside him felt shredded.

"Frank—"

"You should go." He stood up and walked away from her, his cowboy boots adding loud punctuation marks to his break-up. Behind his closed and locked bedroom door, Frank felt nothing but empty. Hollow. Forgotten.

He'd believed she'd come back in the spring, that she'd choose him over baking. But the fact that she was even considering staying in San Francisco and partnering to open a bakery testified that she wouldn't.

His heart felt like it had been ripped from his body, wrung out, and stuffed back in. He wasn't sure how he could live with a heart in such terrible condition, but somehow it kept pumping. He kept breathing, but each moment carried so much pain, Frank couldn't bear to stand up.

Chapter Eleven

Heidi stared after Frank, sure he'd come back out and tell her he was joking. That of course she shouldn't go, that he loved her, that he'd wait until the end of time for her to decide what to do.

She shook her head, angry at him—and herself. *Of course he won't wait forever*, she told herself as she hurried to the cabin to pack her things. The man was now thirty-one-years-old. He wasn't going to sit around and wait for her to make up her mind about them.

The fact that she wanted him to was completely unfair. She made it out of the cabin and into her truck before her chest shuddered. She slammed the truck into reverse and tore out of his driveway before the first tear fell. She made it back to the paved highway before she had to pull over and park because she was crying so hard.

She rested her head against the steering wheel, at an utter loss as to what to do. Should she go back and make him talk to her? Beg him to reconsider, wait until spring to set her free?

In the end, she flicked the truck into drive and headed down the lonely two-lane highway back to Amarillo. Back to Maggie, who folded her into her embrace and sat with her for the rest of Sunday, who whispered comforting words and welcome advice for what to do next.

The next morning, she met the worried gazes of her parents. They saw her red-rimmed eyes, though she'd tried to disguise them with makeup. Her whole face felt puffy, like she'd had a bad reaction to something.

She had. To the thought of never seeing Frank again, never hearing him laugh, never feeling the strength in his touch as he drew her close and kissed her.

By the time she arrived back in San Francisco, she'd been crying for most of the day. Her heart felt broken into a dozen pieces, and she couldn't even pick them all up and put it back together. Because some of them had been left at Three Rivers. Some in Amarillo. The rest somewhere between here and there.

She'd intended to bake for most of Monday afternoon, but she couldn't. Even baking wouldn't soothe this pain, couldn't erase this ache, meant absolutely nothing if she couldn't call Frank on Sunday evenings and open his letters on Wednesday afternoons.

Time numbed Heidi's wounds, and her accelerated classes made her focus on something besides her own misery. She couldn't get her soufflés to rise properly though, because they required an oven at the exact right temperature and no fiddling once they went in. And she couldn't help but check on them periodically. She wasn't sure why, but she knew her anxiety had something to do with it.

Melanie pulled her aside after one class just before Thanksgiving.

"Heidi, how are you feeling?"

"Just fine." Heidi kept her attention on the counter, wiping in a circular motion though it was clean enough now.

"You seem distracted."

"I'm not."

"You're the only one who hasn't been able to show me a suitable soufflé."

Heidi started nodding and couldn't stop. "I'll practice tonight. I'll get it tomorrow." She wrapped up her kitchen supplies and started unbuttoning her chef's jacket. "Is that all?"

"No," Melanie said gently. "I'm worried about you. You haven't been the same since you went to see your boyfriend. Is everything okay?"

Tears sprang to her eyes. She shook her head and wiped her face before she cried in public. She'd managed to keep her emotions in check when with others—except for when Maggie called. She'd been phoning Heidi every couple of days, instead of just on Fridays. Heidi had appreciated it, but she broke down every time. But she'd kept her composure in front of others, even those at church.

She hadn't been able to find her usual solace at church, but she kept attending anyway, hoping for a miracle, a message, something.

"I'll be fine," Heidi said, finally lifting her eyes to Melanie's. "Thanks for asking." She escaped as fast as her feet would take her, wishing she could run away from her life completely. As she hurried home, for the first time since she'd started baking and pastry school, Heidi wanted to leave San Francisco.

Then do it, she thought as she fumbled with her keys to get into her apartment. She paused. Could she—dared she—leave San Francisco? What would happen with her classes? What if she simply got on a trolley and rode until it didn't go any farther? Who would miss her? When would they realize she was gone?

Feeling small and insignificant, she ducked into her apartment and locked the door behind her. Only one thing in the world had been able to calm her when she'd felt like this previously: Frank's embrace.

And prayer.

She hurried into her bedroom and dropped to her knees, desperate to do something to drive away these feelings of inadequacy and despair.

The following day, Heidi's soufflé turned out correctly. She proudly dusted it with powdered sugar and took it to Melanie's counter in the front.

"Beautiful," Melanie said. "Your practice really paid off."

Heidi smiled, though she hadn't practiced last night. She hadn't been able to do much more than stare at the television and wish for the answers she needed to materialize on the screen. They hadn't.

"So with only three weeks left until the Christmas break, you'll just need to finish your hours—how is that coming?—and complete the check-off list you got at the beginning of the semester." Melanie reached for a pen. "If you've got that today, I can check off the soufflé."

"It's in my binder. Just a minute." Heidi returned to her station and collected her binder full of recipes, notes, lectures, and the dreaded check-off list. Melanie signed by the soufflé and checked Heidi's hours.

"You're about twenty hours behind." Melanie glanced up in alarm. "Were you aware of that?"

Panic sliced through Heidi. She knew she'd fallen a little bit off in her baking practice hours. But twenty? She shook her head, determination pouring through her. "I'll get them done."

"You have three weeks," Melanie reminded her as if Heidi hadn't heard her the first time. She glanced at the paper again. "But I have every confidence you'll get them done." She slid the page back to Heidi. "Bring me the baklava after you perfect it."

Heidi gave her the brightest smile she could muster, which meant it barely curved her lips. She cleaned up her station and headed for the market. She'd need phyllo dough and walnuts to make a decent baklava, and she might as well start there.

Two weeks later, Heidi only had five hours to finish her required baking hours, and an entire Sunday afternoon ahead of her. December on the coast was misty and windy and she clutched her coat closed at the throat as she leaned into the weather to get up the hill to the church. Her mind ran through the delicacies she'd bake that afternoon, and she slipped into the back of the chapel unnoticed. She hadn't been sitting by Damon for the past several weeks as she considered his offer to partner with him. He hadn't pushed her, or even asked again, but it had been the core of Heidi's thoughts since Frank had said, "You do your bakery, and I'll run my ranch."

The hymn started, and she listened to the other people sing about the Savior. A sense of peace she hadn't felt in so long descended on her, and she wept with joy. The pastor got up to speak, and Heidi forgot about her baking.

"Great sacrifices require great faith," he said. With those five words, Heidi sat up a little straighter. Maggie had said she'd need to rely on her faith to see her through this trial. Heidi had believed her, but everything seemed shrouded in darkness and she didn't know which way to step.

"Faith can feel elusive," the pastor continued. "But we must ask the Lord to help us have the faith we need, for it is only through our faith that a light can shine in darkness."

Heidi felt the truth of the pastor's words all the way down in her toes. And she decided to employ every ounce of faith that she possessed in order to get an answer to her question.

Lord, *she prayed.* Should I partner with Damon on his bakery? Or go back to Three Rivers and Frank Ackerman?

She honestly didn't know what she wanted anymore, and she just needed a hint, a push, in the right direction. With clarity, she knew she wanted to do what was right for her.

My desires aside, *she continued.* What would Thou have me do?

She would sacrifice whatever was necessary. As if struck by lightning, Heidi heard a voice as plain as day.

You will have a bakery someday. Trust in my timing and judgment.

Her heart pumped out several extra beats. God had just

promised her that her dreams of owning a bakery would come true—according to His timetable.

"Frank," she whispered, her heart taking courage and a true smile gracing her lips. She left the chapel as soon as the pastor finished speaking, not even staying for the closing hymn. Once home, she dialed Frank's number, her fingers shaking and her heart thundering like a herd of wild horses.

He didn't answer, and she hung up, crestfallen. She moved into her kitchen and started preparing a chocolate mousse she'd take over to Damon that evening. She needed to tell him she wouldn't be partnering with him. Though a nervous vein squirreled through her, the weight that had been sitting on her shoulders for almost two months had disappeared.

She hummed like she used as she melted chocolate and whipped the egg yolks with heavy cream. Her heart felt full, like it had broken free of the constraints she'd put it in all those months ago.

With a firm mousse and her courage in place, she walked the few short blocks to Damon's. He answered the door with, "Afternoon, Heidi," and a smile at her dessert. "What'd you make?"

"Chocolate mousse."

He stepped back to let her in. "You almost done with your hours?"

"I have four more," she said as she went into his apartment.

He collapsed on his couch. "Can you believe we only have a few more months of this?" He exhaled and wiped his hand through his hair. "I'll be glad when it's done. I'm tired."

She flashed him a tight smile. "I'm…I'm not coming back in

January."

He turned his head toward her slowly, almost as if he couldn't get it to move through the air. "What?"

"I'm headed home at the end of the week." She needed to cancel her lease, find boxes, get everything shipped, talk to her parents.... "I can't partner with you on the bakery, Damon. I'm sorry."

He waved his hand like that was the least of his worries. "You can't quit pastry school, Heidi."

Her emotions bubbled to the surface, and her exasperation nearly bled into her voice. "Why not?"

"Because you're three classes away from graduating."

She shook her head. "Doesn't matter."

"You're the best pastry chef I've ever met."

Her chin wobbled. "I'll leave this mousse in your fridge, then." She moved into his kitchen and pulled open the fridge. He had hardly anything to eat inside, leaving lots of room for the mousse.

When she returned to the living room, he stood in her way. "Heidi."

"It's the right thing to do," she told him, her voice barley loud enough to cross the distance between them.

"What is?"

"I'm going back to Texas. My heart is there. Frank's there."

"He can wait—"

"I got the confirmation I needed," she said. "Going back is what God wants me to do."

Damon pressed his lips together. "I don't know how to argue with that." He looked at her with pleading in his expression.

"You're four months away. Three classes."

"I know it doesn't make sense."

"No, it doesn't."

She smiled, her anxiety and doubt gone. "But I also know it's the right thing to do. I have *faith* that it is."

He stepped toward her, a smile forming on his face too. "Who should I ask to partner with me, then?"

"Oh, you mean who's second best?"

He laughed. "Richard?"

"Sure, Richard's a great pastry chef."

Damon sighed, a defeated sound. "All right. I'll miss you in the program. And at church."

She gave him a quick hug. "I'll miss you too, Damon. You've been a good friend to me." She left his apartment, and strode home as fast as her legs could carry her. After all, she had dozens of things to do to be ready to move back to Texas in only six days—and at the top of her list?

Call Frank until he answered.

The phone rang as Frank entered the homestead on Sunday evening, but with his hands covered in mud, he didn't answer it. He really needed a second pair of hands, but with his father in town and his brothers off at school, he was left to deal with the sprinklers in the yard. And they'd frozen last night and then cracked this morning, gushing water everywhere.

Frank had managed to fix them with the spare pipes he had in the shed, but he'd missed church, missed lunch, and nearly missed dinner to do it. He was tired, and hungry, and in no mood to speak to anyone. Which meant it was probably best that he'd missed whoever had called.

If he was being honest, he'd been in a foul temper since his birthday, since he'd ended his relationship with Heidi, since he'd been looking for someone else to date and potentially marry. But no one in Three Rivers remotely interested him, and he'd decided he'd be happier a bachelor for the rest of his life than with someone other than Heidi.

But he hadn't felt happy in months. He had moments of contentment, sure. A fleeting feeling of peace during a sermon. A smile during a meeting for his new general controller, or a cowboy as he said good morning. But never true happiness like he'd known when he held Heidi's hand, or kissed her under the stars, or pictured her baking in the kitchen she'd practically designed for his homestead.

Without her here, the ranch felt emptier than it had previously. He'd never feel the same, he knew. She'd changed him, and he didn't know how to be the person he was before. He didn't want to be that person. But he didn't like who he was now either.

"Stop tryin' to analyze everything," he told himself as he scrubbed mud from his hands and under his nails. He'd thought he'd start to feel better with time, but after two months and the pain still as fresh, the wounds still raw, he suspected it would take years for him to get over Heidi.

But that was more analyzing, and Frank didn't have time for

that. Though it was Sunday, with the sprinkler setback, he hadn't made it out to the horse barn yet. With darkness fast approaching, he dried his hands and hurried back out the door. He'd gotten a new horse over the Thanksgiving weekend, and he had to be trained every day.

Frank found comfort in the familiar motions, in the steadiness of the animal. "Hey there, Squirt."

The horse, a gray spotted Arabian, snorted and tossed his head. Frank led him to the fenced circle, where a pole with a plastic bag lay in the dirt. The horse trotted away from Frank and kept his back to him, like he'd been doing for the past couple of weeks since coming to the ranch.

Frank just needed Squirt to trust him. To want to be in the center of the circle with him instead of on the fence line. He picked up the pole and shook the bag, alarming the horse into a trot around the circumference of the pen.

He clicked his tongue and kept his face toward the horse at all times, moving with him in the circle. Eventually Squirt would tire and come into the center. He'd been doing it more and more quickly each day, and Frank hoped that this week, he'd be able to take Squirt to the circle and have him stay in the center.

Only two times around, and Squirt slowed to a walk. After a few strides, he came in close to Frank, his head bowed and his trust complete. Frank dropped the pole, and Squirt stepped right over the plastic bag that usually antagonized him.

"There you go." Frank ran his hand up the horse's nose to his ears. "Right here." He moved, wanting Squirt to follow him, which the horse did. A supreme sense of satisfaction sang through Frank, and he supposed he could feel happiness when he trained his horses. He opened the gate and stepped into the open air, Squirt right at his heels. Frank wandered down the path, through the horse barn, and over to the homestead. The horse came with him every step of the way, no reigns or bridle necessary.

He paused on the threshold of the yard, his boots still on gravel. He'd transformed the house into the kind of homestead a woman could be happy with. Everything about it was new, and modern, and open, and perfect. He'd cleaned up the yard, put in a sprinkling system, built a shed for storage, cleared a spot of land for a vegetable garden, anything to fill his extra time and improve his property.

Squirt nudged Frank's hand with his nose, and Frank petted the horse. "Yeah," he said. "Let's go to the barn." He turned his back on the homestead he'd spent the better part of six months building, wishing he could leave it all behind.

The week passed, as weeks did, and Frank didn't spend more than five or six hours in the house. He couldn't stand to be there alone, surrounded by so much space. At least outside, he could breathe fresh air and feel a sense of freedom. The walls he'd built—though improved and providing a better space—made him feel trapped.

Early Sunday morning, just as the sun started to rise, he took Squirt to the pen, but he didn't immediately trot to the opposite fence, his back to Frank. Instead, the horse stayed right by Frank's side, his soft snuffle the indication that he was ready for the next part of his training.

So Frank saddled the horse and led him around the holding pen, glad the weather had warmed the slightest bit. The air still held a definite chill, and Frank needed his wool jacket, but it hadn't rained, and that made for easier horse training in the outdoor yards.

After an hour or so, Frank returned Squirt to his stall and went to get ready for church. He'd almost stopped going after Heidi had returned to San Francisco, angry at God for allowing her to leave. Then Frank had come to realize that Heidi could make her own choices, and God wasn't going to force anyone to do anything.

He'd returned to church after only a couple of weeks away, but he still felt like somewhat of an imposter entering the chapel and taking a seat next to Chase. "Maggie comin' today?"

"She's in the restroom."

Frank slid back toward the aisle to leave her room. Seeing Maggie sliced through Frank's defenses, not that they were very strong to begin with. But she had the same lines in her face that Heidi did, the same honey-colored hair. Her eyes were lighter, more on the blue spectrum than Heidi's brown, and that alone had allowed Frank to speak with Maggie instead of running from her.

The organ began and the pastor got up just as Maggie slipped into the row. "Sorry." She glanced at Frank and froze, her eyes widening to the size of golf balls. "Frank," she whispered.

"Hey, Maggie."

His voice seemed to unlock her muscles and she sank onto the bench between him and Chase. She leaned over and whispered something to her boyfriend, and Frank wanted to bolt. He hated seeing other couples so happily in love. All it did was awaken the jealousy in him, and he didn't like the negative feelings that came with it.

He made it through the opening hymn before he stood and strode down the aisle toward the lobby. He burst through the doors, his chest nearly on fire for want of oxygen. Stumbling outside, he sucked at the winter air, grateful for the sting of it as it coated his lungs with ice.

He set his feet to walking, hoping it would clear his mind, erase his anxiety, bring Heidi home.

Exhausted after his two-hour walk through, around, and back through town, Frank finally made it back to his truck in the now-empty church parking lot. He climbed into the cab and sat with his hands on the steering wheel. He didn't want to go home.

In the end, he had nowhere else to go, so he set his truck north and drove slowly. When he pulled around the bend, he noticed a truck parked in his driveway. He knew that truck….

When his beautiful Heidi stood from her spot on his front steps, Frank slammed on his brakes. He stared at her across the distance, through the windshield. Had he hallucinated her? Was she really there? How? Why?

She wore a navy skirt and a yellow blouse, all of which billowed in her wake as she moved down the steps and advanced toward him. She exuded confidence and strength—everything Frank hadn't felt since she'd left.

He couldn't get himself to get out of the truck, and she came all the way to him. She opened the door and said, "You really need to invest in an answering machine," followed by a coy smile.

So many emotions streamed through him. Words he'd longed to say crowded into the back of his throat. He simply looked at her, drinking her in, memorizing her so he could recall her in the quiet moments just before he fell asleep.

"Where you been?" she asked, her gaze wandering to the ranch beyond the house. "Everyone else returned from church an hour ago."

"Walking," he managed to croak out.

"Want to walk with me?" she asked. "I have some things I need to tell you." She met his eyes, and he saw a myriad of emotions in hers.

"Sure, yeah." He unbuckled his seat belt. "Yes."

She backed up to give him room to get out, and though he wanted to sweep her into his arms and beg her to forgive him, he tucked his hands into his coat pockets and moved with her when she stepped.

It seemed like a lifetime passed before she spoke. "Frank," she started. "I quit pastry school."

His feet froze. "You did what now?"

She moved in front of him, her cheeks pink from the cold and her eyes as bright as he'd ever seen them. "I quit pastry school. I'm not going back to San Francisco. I moved back to Amarillo." She scuffed her feet in the dirt. "I'm hoping to move back to Three Rivers really soon."

Confusion and disbelief and absolute joy warred for placement in his chest. "I don't get it," he blurted.

"Let me explain it to you." She reached toward him, and he removed one of his hands from its pocket to take hers in his. Everything inside him relaxed, reveled, rejoiced at her touch. He needed to listen to her, find out what she'd done, and then figure out how to keep her in his life for good.

Chapter Twelve

Heidi wasn't sure if Frank just needed more time to absorb what she'd told him, or if he didn't quite know how to word his thoughts, or if he never wanted to see her again. She'd definitely surprised him, but it wasn't her fault the man didn't own an answering machine or answer his phone when it rang.

He'd said he'd spent little time in the house this week, and with his sincere apology, she'd believed him. He'd let her hold his hand, but he'd pulled it back the longer they walked, the longer she talked.

But she wanted him to know everything. Everything that she'd felt when he broke up with her. Everything she'd thought about, prayed about, worried about. Everything she'd been through as she struggled to make her decision.

And now.... Now Frank hadn't spoken in at least ten minutes, his eyes trained on the ground at his cowboy boots and the wind kicking up into gusts. They'd looped the ranch buildings three times, and as she faced the open range to the east of the homestead, she felt braver than she ever had.

"I'll go," she said when her truck came into view. "You can call me when you're ready."

His hand landed heavily on her forearm. "Don't go."

"You haven't said anything."

He turned toward her, and she let him shield her from the worst of the wind, wanting him to protect her from all of life's storms. Tentatively, almost like he had the first time he'd touched her, he drew her into his arms. She gladly went, tears gathering in her eyes at his tenderness, his forgiveness.

"I love you, Heidi," he whispered into her hair. "I will do everything I can to make sure you get your bakery one day."

She held him tightly, the words she wanted to tell him springing to her vocal chords. "You are worth more than any bakery."

She felt the smile on his face as he brought his lips to hers, true joy bursting through her like she'd never known.

"So I still need a cleaning person," he whispered as he tracked his lips across her jaw. "You interested?"

"I don't know." She shivered in the cold, but also because of Frank's delicious touch. "What's the boss like?"

He tipped his head back and laughed, the sound fleeing into the stormy sky and getting swallowed by the wind. "Well, he's been really moody and unpleasant for the past couple of months." He tucked his hand in hers and led her toward the homestead. "But I think things are going to start to get better now."

Only a few days later, Heidi once again loaded everything she owned into the back of her father's truck. This time she wasn't headed to the post office to ship it to San Francisco. As Maggie drove, Heidi let the miles roll by in silence. When they pulled into the outskirts of town, Heidi said, "You know, I never said thank you."

"For what?" Maggie glanced at her out of the corner of her eye.

"For telling me I had great faith." Heidi took a deep breath, feeling stronger than she ever had. "I'd never really felt that way about myself. But when I needed it, my faith was there." She threw a smile in her sister's direction. "And that's because of you."

"Well, I don't know how much I did."

"You've always been right about Frank," Heidi said. "I shouldn't have told him about the bakery, and I should've had more faith to do what God wanted me to." She looked out the window as Main Street went by. "I got there, but it was a harder path."

"As long as you got there."

Frank met them in the parking lot at the ranch, and he had his wranglers carry Heidi's things back to her cabin. She smiled and hugged them, hugged them and smiled. And she knew without a trace of doubt that she was back where she was supposed to be. Her muscles relaxed; her worries fled.

Finally. She was home.

Christmas approached, and Heidi didn't have a gift for Frank. She had no way of getting him a gift—at least not if she wanted it to be a surprise. He spent nearly every waking minute with her, claiming that ranching in the winter wasn't nearly as much work.

It was, and Heidi knew it, but she enjoyed her time with Frank, knowing that he'd get done what needed to get done.

She considered sewing him a new shirt, but her fabric all felt too feminine to her. She almost asked Chase to drive her into town, but she couldn't think of a plausible reason that wouldn't raise Frank's suspicions. Perhaps she should simply take him shopping in Amarillo when they went to visit her family and eat Christmas Eve dinner.

With that plan in place, she put the matter from her mind. Finally, the day arrived that they'd travel to Amarillo with Frank knocking on her door at mid-morning. "You ready?"

She smoothed down her blouse and wished her leggings didn't itch so much. "Sure am." She smiled at him and leaned into his kiss. He seemed nervous, distracted, and he pulled away sooner than she liked. "You okay?"

"Fine," he said, but he didn't sound fine. He grabbed her suitcase, and they walked hand-in-hand to his truck, and the drive to Amarillo was filled with nice conversation. She had to work harder to keep his attention, and again she wondered what had him so preoccupied.

"You missed the turn," she said, looking behind her as the street that led to her house passed.

"We're goin' somewhere first."

"Where?"

He shifted in his seat. "I don't wanna say."

"Frank," she warned, a smile curling her lips. "Tell me where we're goin'."

He slid her a flirtatious grin. "I like it when you talk like a cowgirl."

"Frank."

"Heidi."

She nudged her shoulder into his. "Tell me." But he turned, and the jewelry store loomed in front of her. "Frank," she breathed.

"I don't have a Christmas gift for you," he said, his words now rushing over themselves. "But I figured a wedding ring would be sufficient." He slid her a glance, but he couldn't look long.

Heidi didn't know what to say. Her breath stuck somewhere in her chest as he pulled into the parking lot and stopped. She turned toward him as he fully focused on her, the attentive, intense Frank she'd known for six months finally back.

"I love you, Heidi Duffin, and I spoke to your father on the phone last night. I have his blessing to marry you. I'm just—" He cleared his throat in a rare show of nerves. "I guess I'm just wondering if you'd like to marry me."

She wasn't sure if she wanted to receive her proposal in the cab of his truck. Then again, she'd fallen in love with him in simple circumstances, and some of her favorite times with him had happened right here in this truck.

She blinked, and he did too, his bright eyes so full of hope, of happiness, of a beautiful future they could have together.

"Yes," she whispered, her voice scratching her throat.

A smile burst onto his face, but he said, "I didn't quite hear you."

"Yes!" She threw her arms around him and kissed him.

He chuckled and gazed down at her. "All right, then. Let's go get a ring."

The End

Read on to the first chapter of Liz's new inspirational western romance series, BEFORE THE LEAP, a Gold Valley Romance, Book 1.

before the leap

one

The chilled bite of the winter wind pulled against Jace Lovell's cowboy hat, causing him to reach up and press one palm firmly on top of his head to keep it in place. A native of Gold Valley, Montana—and now the foreman at Horseshoe Home Ranch that spread partway up one of the mountains that surrounded the valley—Jace understood the weather. Almost like he and Mother Nature had come to an agreement.

But he didn't smile at the drifts of snow along the path leading from his cabin to the administration lodge or the promise of more wet weather. He wasn't planning on smiling at all. Because today, he had to conduct interviews to hire an interior designer to "renovate everything."

Yep, those were the directions he'd received from the ranch owner's wife, Gloria Brush. *Renovate everything.* Cowboy cabins—including his—the administration lodge, even the organization and flow of the tack rooms, and stables, and barns. *Everything*.

And Jace, as foreman, had to sit through an entire day of interviews. Caged between the walls, when he could be feeding cattle, or sweeping out horse stalls, or almost anything but talking to people and sitting in a chair all day.

At least the interior designers were coming to him. He climbed the stairs to the administration lodge—which functioned and looked just fine to him—and pushed through the door. A rush of heated air warmed his skin, driving away the icy chill that had kissed his cheeks. He lifted his hat, ran his fingers through his dark hair, and settled the hat back into place.

The lodge buzzed with activity. In anticipation of the upcoming interviews, he had the boys organizing tables and chairs this morning. He took a deep breath and tried to imagine the spacious building differently. But he didn't have the eye or mind of a designer and couldn't really picture anything that wasn't already there. Surely the designer wouldn't be satisfied with functionality, oh, no. Leave it to Gloria to try to make a cattle ranch feel like a day spa.

Jace wasn't entirely sure why Gloria wanted to remodel, and a skin of worry encased him. Were they preparing to sell Horseshoe Home? What would become of him if they did? He'd just gotten his footing as foreman and he'd grown up on the ranch as his father had been foreman before Jace.

He squared his shoulders and dismissed his rampant worries. He'd ask Gloria why she wanted the renovation the next chance he got. No sense in worrying about it until then.

As he glanced around, he noticed that the carpet was worn, but this was a working ranch with two-dozen cowboys coming and going. The walls had been repainted a bright white just last year. He'd spearheaded that campaign during one of the worst weather weeks Montana had ever witnessed. Besides feeding and watering the livestock, the cowboys stayed indoors. Sixty degrees below zero would do that to a ranch.

The high ceilings bore the skeleton of the majestic wooden structure, with exposed beams slanting toward the pinnacle of the roof. Desks and chairs littered the open space out front, and doorways lined the perimeter. See, the lodge used to be the homestead. So the kitchen had stayed put, but the large dining room had been set up as a break room of sorts, where cowboys could eat lunch or relax.

The bedrooms down the hall functioned as offices for the accountant, the foreman, and the owner. The open living area had become their meeting room, and a few of the cowboys had desks to keep sales reports, folders of information about feed supplies, and whatever else they needed to do their particular job well.

"All set, boss." Landon, the tall former rodeo star approached Jace. "I even had Howie clean the bathrooms."

The owner had a cleaning service come through the lodge every week, but they weren't scheduled to come until Thursday—and that was nowhere near enough with thirty men using the building day in and day out.

"Thanks." Jace made his voice as friendly as he could, because he couldn't get his lips to curve upward. "And we'll be meeting them—" He glanced toward the flurry of activity in the open area to his left. "In my office?"

"You said you didn't care where, and there's a storm blowin' in...." Landon cut a look toward a couple of rowdier cowhands, but they didn't notice. "We'll have the feeding done in an hour and then Rob said we could put on a movie after that while it snows."

Jace fisted his hand so he wouldn't pinch the bridge of his nose. It was only Monday—he had a long week ahead of him, if showing movies was any indication.

"Thought the best place for that was here," Landon said. "But I can—"

"It's fine, Landon." Jace had asked him to get things set up and keep the cowboys busy. "I guess I'll be in my office. Will you show the first applicant back when they arrive?"

"Sure thing, boss," Landon called after him, as Jace had already started walking away. He maneuvered through the maze and escaped down the hall. His office sat through the first door on the right, and a sense of calm prevailed after he shut the door. He closed his eyes and thought, *Help me get through this day.*

He wasn't terribly religious, but since his brother, Tom, had moved back to Gold Valley, Jace had been attending church with him and his family. Maybe some of the pastor's words about prayer had infused into Jace's mind.

No matter what, he felt calmer as he settled behind his desk, ran his hands down his face and over his beard, and opened the first folder. He'd prepared them on Saturday afternoon after he'd de-iced the outdoor watering troughs. He hadn't had a chance to review every applicant, and he probably wouldn't be able to finish that job before the first applicant arrived for her interview.

Jace had known enough to ask for a portfolio from each applicant, and he flipped the page to see what this first one had designed. So many pastels met his eye he wondered if he'd been swallowed by a rainbow. He could not imagine walking into a cowboy cabin only to be greeted by sea green walls and lavender cabinets.

Wild hope that the approaching storm would keep the applicants in town tore through him. Maybe he could put this off until another day. He closed the folder just as someone knocked on the door. Heart sinking, he called, "C'mon in."

The door opened, showing Landon standing just to the side of the doorway. "Right in there, ma'am."

A woman entered, her dark hair plaited, with the end of her braid riding over her shoulder. She wore a professional pantsuit and carried a leather briefcase purse. Sourness stained the back of Jace's throat. She wasn't Wendy, but her clothing and accessory selections reminded him so much of his ex that Jace thought seriously about bolting.

After all, that was what she'd done.

He stuffed his emotions down to the bottom of his steel-tipped cowboy boots and stood. "Hello." He tried not to feel intimidated by her, but the truth was, the feeling that he was outclassed in every sense of the word flowed through him like a fast-moving river.

His panic only increased as the interview commenced. He made it through, told Miss Purple Pastel that he'd let her know very soon, and let her go. He pulled the door closed behind her, and Jace paced back to the window. Sure enough, fat flakes had started to drift down to the ground, adding to the already high piles of snow.

His thoughts fled to Wendy, as they always did when he let his guard down. She'd left him after three years together. Left him standing at the altar by himself—oh, and half the town in attendance. Left him for a more exciting life and career in Los Angeles. Everything about that designer reminded him of Wendy, and for that reason alone—not to mention the horrendous pastels—he couldn't hire her.

Another knock sounded. Another woman entered. Another interview started. Miss Wood Nymph favored dark woods and light, gauzy materials. Jace wondered if such curtains would withstand a single day against twenty-four cowhands.

Miss Giddy bubbled into the room with giggles and grins, spoke the same way, and left in a cloud of expensive-smelling perfume. By lunch, Jace knew today was shaping up to be the worst day he'd ever experienced on the ranch. And he hated that, because the ranch was his safe haven. The one place Wendy hadn't permeated, hadn't poisoned, hadn't permanently altered in his life.

Three more interviews, and still Jace didn't see something in the folders—or the applicants—he thought might fit at Horseshoe Home. Finally, only one folder remained on his desk. He didn't bother to open it. All the designers had brought a copy of their designs for the different spaces on the ranch.

Landon opened the door and said, "Miss Belle."

Jace snapped his head up, ice sinking through his chest, coating his lungs and internal organs in stiff blocks he'd never escape. Why hadn't—?

"Well, look at you." Belle strode forward, her luxurious auburn hair flowing behind her like a curtain. She'd pinned back only the very front, leaving the rest to frame her high cheekbones, her bright green eyes, and her very glossed lips.

Jace yanked his attention away from those lips, which had always intrigued him. "Look at me?" he asked, making a conscious effort not to reach up and smooth down his beard like he did when he wanted to look his best. "Look at *you*. What happened? Did Sacramento run out of red lipstick? You had to come all the way to Gold Valley to get stocked up?"

"Ha ha." She swept him from head to toe. "I see you're still wearing that ridiculous hat."

"Everyone wears these hats," he shot back. "We're cowboys."

"Yes, well, most *decent* men buy a replacement every few years." She sniffed as she perched on the edge of the chair across from his desk and pulled a folder from her purse. No briefcase bag. No pretentious heels—Belle didn't need them. She stood almost as tall as her brother, Landon.

The snake, Jace thought as he rounded the desk and took his seat. Landon should've told him his sister had applied. Growing up, Jace had never seen eye-to-eye with the redhead, though he did enjoy trading jabs with her when she visited from her hoity-toity job at a design firm in Sacramento.

Instead of focusing on her tight black jeans and flowing top of cobalt blue—which he thought made her hair look positively decadent—he flipped open the folder to check her address. "You moved back?"

She shrugged one shoulder, the silky blouse she wore slipping a little. "My parents are on a six-month service mission in Africa. I'm taking care of the house."

He returned his gaze to the folder, which was safer than drinking in Belle's curves. "Mm hm." He'd heard that before. Pretty princess left home, and instead of admitting that the world had chewed her up, she came home "to take care of the house."

"You must be tired." Her tone, which someone less experienced than Jace could've misinterpreted to be sympathetic, caused him to abandon the folder.

"Why do you say that?" Jace knew Belle's body didn't actually house sympathetic bones, even though she dressed it up nice and sprayed intoxicating, lilac-scented perfume across her collarbone. His gaze dropped to that spot, and her golden skin made his blood run a little faster.

"You didn't even make a joke about me taking care of the house."

Jace opened his mouth to say something, but closed it when nothing came to mind. "It's been a long day. Let's get this over with." With effort, he closed her folder and shoved his traitorous thoughts about Belle's attractiveness to the back of his mind. "Did you bring your portfolio?"

Belle's stomach flipped and flopped like a fish someone had left to die on the shore. Jace took forever to look at her portfolio, and he knew it. Was enjoying making her wait on him—just like he always had. At least not everything in Belle's world had exploded when she'd lost her job in Sacramento. It only felt that way, especially being back in her hometown and having to see everyone who'd never left.

"What's the last thing you worked on?" he asked, the slow rumble of his voice sending a shiver through her body.

Belle smiled, and it actually felt real on her face. "I did an old ranch-style house near the Redwoods. Beautiful setting. Trees everywhere. Lots of natural wood." She slid an oversized sheet toward him. The vibrant photos didn't do the place justice. She'd loved that property, the serenity she'd felt in those woods. In truth, she'd been hoping to recapture some of those feelings in Gold Valley, which boasted of the same slow pace of life, similar mountains and trees and peace.

"This is nice, Belle." He glanced up at her. Not long enough to truly make eye contact, but she heard the sincerity in his voice. She basked in the compliment, as she hadn't had many in a long time.

"Nice?" came out of her mouth. She cursed her quick wit—and Jace Lovell. He seemed to bring out the sharpest edge to her tongue.

His eyes came up more slowly this time and sank into hers. She could lose herself in the deep, dark depths of them—if she were anywhere close to even thinking about dating a man. And even if she was, he would most certainly not be a rancher, a friend of her brother's, or Jace Lovell. Three strikes against him.

He's out, she told herself firmly.

Still, he had beautiful eyes. And a full beard she wanted to trace her fingers through. "It's more than nice. That's gorgeous work."

"Gorgeous?" He turned the paper over as if there'd be evidence of gorgeousness on the back. "I guess you're the expert." He put it unceremoniously in the folder and closed the file. "I'll let you know soon."

"How many applicants did you have?" She leaned back and crossed her legs. Just because he was the interviewer didn't mean she couldn't ask some of her own questions.

He stared at her, and she didn't entirely hate the way his gaze seemed to see past all of her carefully crafted defenses. "'Bout eight, I reckon."

"You reckon?" She laughed. "It's a number," she said. "It's either seven, or eight, or nine. There's no guessing at it."

He came around the desk and sat on the edge of it, his powerful presence combined with the delicious scent of his cologne nearly knocking Belle backward. She straightened her spine to maintain her position, especially when he crossed those enormous arms. He must eat a pound of meat for every meal to keep muscles like that.

"Since we're keeping track of torture," he growled. "Eight."

"Are any of them better than me?"

"All of 'em."

Her heart sank, though she knew Jace had only said that to rub at her. Maybe he had seen her extreme insecurity when he stared at her. She swallowed hard, trying to find her center and pull all her masks back in place.

Finally, she stood and tossed her purse strap over her shoulder. "Well, it's been a pleasure, Mister Lovell." She made her voice sticky sweet and as Southern as possible. She flounced toward the door, turning back with her hand on the knob. "You still oiling your beard?"

She didn't wait for him to answer. She flung him a smirk and practically ran from his office before he could respond. Ooh, that'd make him mad. A tug of regret pulled through her, but she couldn't afford for him to see anything but the powerhouse Belle had been when she'd gone off to Sacramento to conquer the world.

Belle noticed the traveling eyes of the cowboys who watched her as she wove through the desks, tables, and chairs toward the exit. Landon had kept them all at bay since she'd returned to Gold Valley two weeks ago.

Isn't that just like Jace not to know I'd come home? she thought as she faced the winter storm. Indignation filled her, marred by a tiny part of her that simply felt wounded. Sure, she and Jace weren't going to text and hang out, but she considered him a friend. Maybe not a close one, or one she actually wanted to spend much time with, but at least someone who should've known she'd come back.

As she drove along the sloppy ruts in the road toward civilization, she remembered that she hadn't seen him at all either. Not at church, though she'd only gone once and sat in the balcony so she could escape quicker. Not in town. Nowhere. Landon had told her he was the foreman now, so maybe that kept him busier than she would have thought.

Please help me get this job. Her fingers turned white from her death grip on the steering wheel, and a rush of fear made her wish she could recall her poisoned words about Jace's beard. Even if he did oil it, she shouldn't have said so—not if she wanted to get the job. She turned back onto the paved, snow-plowed highway and headed for the town of Gold Valley, her mind churning.

Maybe she should go back. Apologize about the beard comment. Her mouth turned dry at the thought of maybe tracing her fingertips along Jace's jaw.... Her phone chimed as she made it out of the canyon. Six texts from her new supervisor at the design firm had come in at the same time. She realized she didn't have cell service in the canyon or up at the ranch, and hurried to call him back.

"Hey, Calvin," she said when he answered.

"Where have you been? The samples for the Montgomery cabin came in, and I need you here."

"You sent me out to Horseshoe Home Ranch." The saucy side of Belle almost added, "Remember?" but she managed to swallow the word back before it came out. She would've said it to Jace, but Calvin was as far from Jace as someone could get. He wouldn't appreciate it—but he didn't have the authority to cut her loose because of it.

"Oh, right." Shuffling came through the line, and Belle suspected his attention had already shifted to something else. "How did it go?"

"Great," Belle said, hoping she wasn't fibbing. "He said I'd know soon."

"I hope so," Calvin said. "You need to book a client."

I know, she wanted to scream. Calvin had made his opinion of her very clear, and he wasn't impressed. She came with no loyal clients, no prospects, no accounts, and hardly any experience. A year in the Sacramento firm, where she'd basically been an intern to the top designer there, hadn't exactly catapulted her career.

"I feel good about it." Her voice sounded false and too bright to her own ears.

"Feeling good about something doesn't mean much."

"I'll be back to the office in a few minutes." One glance at the clock on her dashboard told her she should've finished work fifteen minutes ago. But when Calvin called....

"No need," he said. "We'll go over these samples first thing in the morning. Don't forget my coffee." He hung up before Belle could confirm.

Steam practically leaked from her ears. She was his colleague, not his secretary. She paid for her own desk space, same as he did. He brought in more money to the conglomerate, sure. But that didn't mean she had to bring him coffee. In fact, he'd "asked" her several times to bring him a cappuccino, and each time she'd "forgotten."

She'd "forget" tomorrow too, even though her forgetfulness probably lowered his opinion of her. "Can't get much lower," she muttered to herself as she rounded the corner and came face-to-face with the horseshoe-shaped waterfalls. Past them, she finally saw the outskirts of town ahead.

Belle didn't care. She wasn't going to take the guy coffee. She'd land the account at Horseshoe Home, and start saving to open her own design company. She knew she was a good designer—better than anyone else in Gold Valley. She'd signed on with the design firm for legitimacy, to have a name to put on her business cards, but she dreamed of having her name speak for itself, her own name on her stationery, on the side of a building.

She prayed again for help from the Lord as the desperation to accomplish all she hoped to do crowded her lungs and made her gasp for air.

BEFORE THE LEAP is available now. Look for it at your favorite retailer.

Read all the books in the Three Rivers Ranch Romance series!

Second Chance Ranch: A Three Rivers Ranch Romance (Book 1): After his deployment, injured and discharged Major Squire Ackerman returns to Three Rivers Ranch, wanting to forgive Kelly for ignoring him a decade ago. He'd like to provide the stable life she needs, but with old wounds opening and a ranch on the brink of financial collapse, it will take patience and faith to make their second chance possible.

Third Time's the Charm: A Three Rivers Ranch Romance (Book 2): First Lieutenant Peter Marshall has a truckload of debt and no way to provide for a family, but Chelsea helps him see past all the obstacles, all the scars. With so many unknowns, can Pete and Chelsea develop the love, acceptance, and faith needed to find their happily ever after?

Fourth and Long: A Three Rivers Ranch Romance (Book 3): Commander Brett Murphy goes to Three Rivers Ranch to find some rest and relaxation with his Army buddies. Having his ex-wife show up with a seven-year-old she claims is his son is anything but the R&R he craves. Kate needs to make amends, and Brett needs to find forgiveness, but are they too late to find their happily ever after?

Fifth Generation Cowboy: A Three Rivers Ranch Romance (Book 4): Tom Lovell has watched his friends find their true happiness on Three Rivers Ranch, but everywhere he looks, he only sees friends. Rose Reyes has been bringing her daughter out to the ranch for equine therapy for months, but it doesn't seem to be working. Her challenges with Mari are just as frustrating as ever. Could Tom be exactly what Rose needs? Can he remove his friendship blinders and find love with someone who's been right in front of him all this time?

Sixth Street Love Affair: A Three Rivers Ranch Romance Novella: After losing his wife a few years back, Garth Ahlstrom thinks he's ready for a second chance at love. But Juliette Thompson has a secret that could destroy their budding relationship. Can they find the strength, patience, and faith to make things work?

Get this digital-only novella for free when you join Liz's newsletter!

The Seventh Sergeant: A Three Rivers Ranch Romance (Book 5): Discharged from the Army and now with a good job at Courage Reins, Sergeant Reese Sanders has finally found a new version of happiness—until a horrific fall puts him right back where he was years ago: Injured and depressed. Down-on-her luck Carly Watters despises small towns almost as much as she loathes cowboys. But she finds herself faced with both when she gets assigned to Reese's case. Do Reese and Carly have the humility and faith to make their relationship more than professional?

Eight Second Ride: A Three Rivers Ranch Romance (Book 6): Ethan Greene loves his work at Three Rivers Ranch, but he can't seem to find the right woman to settle down with. When sassy yet vulnerable Brynn Bowman shows up at the ranch to recruit him back to the rodeo circuit, he takes a different approach with the barrel racing champion. His patience and newfound faith pay off when a friendship--and more--starts with Brynn. But she wants out of the rodeo circuit right when Ethan wants to rejoin. Can they find the path God wants them to take and still stay together?

Christmas in Three Rivers: A Three Rivers Ranch Romance Novella Collection: Isn't Christmas the best time to fall in love? The cowboys of Three Rivers Ranch think so. Join four of them as they journey toward their path to happily ever after in four, all-new novellas in the Amazon #1 Bestselling Three Rivers Ranch Romance series.

THE NINTH INNING: The Christmas season has never felt like such a burden to boutique owner Andrea Larsen. But with Mama gone and the holidays upon her, Andy finds herself wishing she hadn't been so quick to judge her former boyfriend, cowboy Lawrence Collins. Well, Lawrence hasn't forgotten about Andy either, and he devises a plan to get her out to the ranch so they can reconnect. Do they have the faith and humility to patch things up and start a new relationship?

TEN DAYS IN TOWN: Sandy Keller is tired of the dating scene in Three Rivers. Though she owns the pancake house, she's looking for a fresh start, which means an escape from the town where she grew up. When her older brother's best friend, Tad Jorgensen, comes to town for the holidays, it is a balm to his weary soul. A helicopter tour guide who experienced a near-death experience, he's looking to start over too--but in Three Rivers. Can Sandy and Tad navigate their troubles to find the path God wants them to take--and discover true love--in only ten days?

ELEVEN YEAR REUNION: Pastry chef extraordinaire, Grace Lewis has moved to Three Rivers to help Heidi Ackerman open a bakery in Three Rivers. Grace relishes the idea of starting over in a town where no one knows about her failed cupcakery. She doesn't expect to run into her old high school boyfriend, Jonathan Carver. A carpenter working at Three Rivers Ranch, Jon's in town against his will. But with Grace now on the scene, Jon's thinking life in Three Rivers is suddenly looking up. But with her focus on baking and his disdain for small towns, can they make their eleven year reunion stick?

THE TWELFTH TOWN: Newscaster Taryn Tucker has had enough of life on-screen. She's bounced from town to town before arriving in Three Rivers, completely alone and completely anonymous--just the way she now likes it. She takes a job cleaning at Three Rivers Ranch, hoping for a chance to figure out who she is and where God wants her. When she meets happy-go-lucky cowhand Kenny Stockton, she doesn't expect sparks to fly. Kenny's always been "the best friend" for his female friends, but the pull between him and Taryn can't be denied. Will they have the courage and faith necessary to make their opposite worlds mesh?

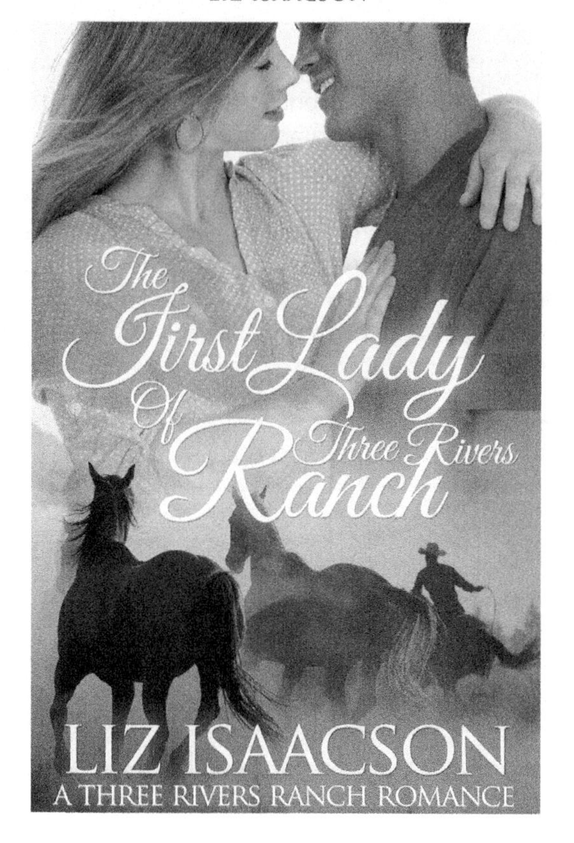

The First Lady of Three Rivers Ranch: A Three Rivers Ranch Romance (Book 7): Heidi Duffin has been dreaming about opening her own bakery since she was thirteen years old, and now she only has one year left before she's a certified pastry chef. She's home for the summer when she goes to Three Rivers with her sister--and meets Frank Ackerman. He convinces Heidi to come clean the cowboy cabins, but the siren's call of a bakery is still loud in Heidi's ears, even if she's also seeing a future with Frank. Can she rely on her faith in ways she's never had to before or will their relationship end when summer does?

Lucky Number Thirteen: A Three Rivers Ranch Romance Novella: Tanner Wolf, a rodeo champion ten times over, is excited to be riding in Three Rivers for the first time since he left his philandering ways and found religion—until a terrible accident lands him in the hospital. Because she's been burned in the past, nurse Summer Hamblin is the queen of first dates, but if she wants to find a way to make a relationship with the transient rodeo star work, she'll have to go on a second date. Can they find love among the tragedy?

Before the Leap: A Gold Valley Romance (Book 1): Jace Lovell only has one thing left after his fiancé abandons him at the altar: his job at Horseshoe Home Ranch. Belle Edmunds is back in Gold Valley and she's desperate to build a portfolio that she can use to start her own firm in Montana. Jace isn't anywhere near forgiving his fiancé, and he's not sure he's ready for a new relationship with someone as fiery and beautiful as Belle. Can she employ her patience while he figures out how to forgive so they can find their own brand of happily-ever-after?

After the Fall: A Gold Valley Romance (Book 2): Professional snowboarder Sterling Maughan has sequestered himself in his family's cabin in the exclusive mountain community above Gold Valley, Montana after a devastating fall that ended his career. Norah Watson cleans Sterling's cabin and the more time they spend together, the more Sterling is interested in all things Norah. As his body heals, so does his faith. Will Norah be able to trust Sterling so they can have a chance at true love?

Through the Mist: A Gold Valley Romance (Book 3): Landon Edmunds has been a cowboy his whole life. An accident five years ago ended his successful rodeo career, and now he's looking to start a horse ranch--and he's looking outside of Montana. Which would be great if God hadn't brought Megan Palmer back to Gold Valley right when Landon is looking to leave. Megan and Landon work together well, and as sparks fly, she's sure God brought her back to Gold Valley so she could find her happily ever after. Through serious discussion and prayer, can Landon and Megan find their future together?

Liz Isaacson writes inspirational romance, usually set in Texas, or Montana, or anywhere else horses and cowboys exist. She lives in Utah, where she teaches elementary school, taxis her daughter to dance several times a week, and eats a lot of Ferrero Rocher while writing.

Find her on her website at lizisaacson.com.

She also writes as Elana Johnson, who is the author of the young adult *Possession* series, the new adult futuristic fantasy *Elemental* series, and two contemporary novels-in-verse, ELEVATED and SOMETHING ABOUT LOVE. Her debut adult fantasy, ECHOES OF SILENCE, was published by Kindle Press in May 2016. Her debut contemporary romance, UNTIL SUMMER ENDS, was published by Cleis Press in August, 2016.

Made in the USA
Monee, IL
20 October 2022